www.SaucyRomanceBooks.com/RomanceBooks

In Love With The Enemy

A billionaire pregnancy romance with a twist

A complete pregnancy romance, brought to you by top selling author Ashlie Brookes.

For four years, Briar has been stuck in a loveless marriage with Adrian. A marriage that only happened when her father gave her to Adrian as repayment for a large debt.

Twice her age, Adrian has no interest in Briar other than her appearance; she's nothing more than a trophy wife, so their relationship is dead in every way but on paper.

Then Briar meets billionaire Mickey. Mickey, like Adrian, owns and trains racehorses, and just so happens to be Adrian's rival.

AUG 16

Though when he and Briar find each other, there's an instant connection like nothing she's ever felt before. She knows that she shouldn't act on her feelings, even if she's in a marriage neither party really cares about.

But the more she gets to know and becomes attracted to Mickey, the harder that becomes... Will Briar give in to the temptation? And if so, what repercussions will this new relationship have?

Find out in this emotional yet steamy pregnancy romance by Ashlie Brookes of African American Club. Suitable for over 18s only due to hot baby making scenes between a competitive billionaire and his Nubian queen!

Get Free Romance eBooks!

Hi there. As a special thank you for buying this book, for a limited time I want to send you some great ebooks completely **free of charge** directly to your email! You can get it by going to this page:

www.saucyromancebooks.com/physical

You can see a the cover of these books on the next page:

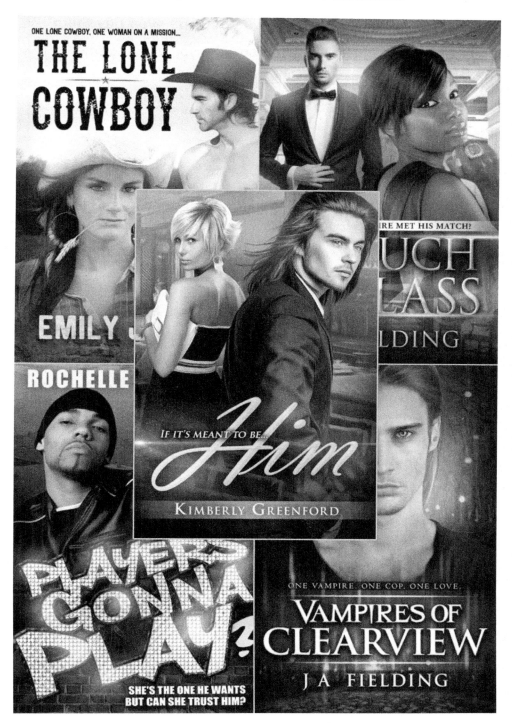

These ebooks are so exclusive you can't even buy them. When you download them I'll also send you updates when new books like this are available.

Again, that link is:

www.saucyromancebooks.com/physical

Contents

Chapter 1

The GPS chimed as the turn loomed up ahead. "Turn left in two tenths of a mile," the synthesized voice of "Karen" urged.

Briar glared at nav screen. "Karen" never sounded like she needed coffee, or a day off. "Karen" never sounded like she was having a bad hair day, either. "Karen" sounded like the perfect woman, the kind who carefully put her makeup on five minutes before her loving husband Bob got home from work and wore pearls to do her vacuuming. "Karen" sounded like a depressingly white stereotype from the nineteen fifties.

Briar bit her lip and cursed at herself. She should have stopped for more coffee, if she was siting here getting irrationally angry at the GPS system. The GPS didn't have a personality. It didn't have an ethnic background, either. It had a pre-recorded voice, and if Briar was getting irritated with that voice the problem probably lay with Briar. Maybe she should have had less coffee, not more.

She took the left that "Karen" directed and tried to force herself to relax. She didn't see what she was getting so tense about. She liked these long, quiet drives. Sure, it was early. Sure, her final destination probably wasn't going to have much to offer, but it wasn't about the destination. Right now Briar had the open road, lined with pretty paddocks and tinted with golden sunlight just starting to peek through the trees. Right now, everything was beautiful.

Briar had grown up in country like this. Of course, if someone had told her ten years ago that she'd be driving a BMW through that same countryside she'd have laughed at them, and probably told them to quit day drinking while they were at it. She chuckled, although there wasn't a lot of humor in the sound.

A beat-up old pickup truck would have been more her speed. Not that she should complain. She had the Beamer, her dad had a new truck by now, and her parents got to stay on their land. All in all, things had worked out more or less okay. She should be grateful.

The track loomed up ahead. Even this early, the site had the full parking staff out in force. Well, that was fine. They had a job to do and so did she. Briar steeled herself and plastered a neutral, pleasant smile onto her face. This was her public mask, the look that she was expected to present every time she showed herself outside the walls of the farm she shared with Adrian. It was a small price to pay, she reminded herself. She could do this, for her family. A smile didn't cost her anything.

The parking attendants guided her into a parking spot. She tried not to get annoyed about that, and then when that failed she tried not to show her annoyance. Maybe they weren't being condescending jerks who didn't think that a woman could park a car all by herself; maybe they were just used to spoiled rich brats who had more concern for the clear coats on their precious cars than they had for their horses. She took a deep breath and forced her temper down before she re-applied her lipstick and slid out of the driver's seat.

She could feel the eyes on her as she strode over to the track entrance. One or two people snapped quick photos, but no one approached so she figured she could live with that. She kept her plastered-on smile as she handed her ticket over to the old man working behind the turnstile, and she bought herself another cup of coffee from the lone concession stand that was open at this hour. Only now, armed with more coffee and a somewhat improved outlook, did she seek out

Worthington Stables' barn.

The barns weren't hard to find. Briar had been around horses

her entire life and she didn't need some usher to give her

directions. A security guard did try to stop her when she set

her sights on the corridor leading back toward the secure area

that housed the horses and their trainers, but his partner held

him back. "Pardon him, ma'am," the partner said, glaring at

the younger guard. "He's new."

Briar didn't say anything. She just gave them a cool,

professional smile and moved on.

She found Adrian easily. He'd spent the night on-site, as had

his workers. Non-horse people, normal people, were

sometimes surprised to find that some owners and trainers did

that before a race, but Briar had done it herself before her

marriage. It was one of the few ways that her husband didn't disappoint her. A lot of people had a lot of money riding on these horses, and it wasn't just the prize money either. Someone planning to bet a lot of money on one horse would certainly not scruple to hurt a different horse to ensure the win. Briar had seen it happen before.

She took a deep breath. Out beyond the chain, the track smelled like cleaning solution and old hot dogs. Back here, she could smell horses and feed. Back here, she could almost imagine herself back at home, or at least at her husband's place. If she closed her eyes, she could just about imagine her father's hired hands just around the corner, bringing in one of the steeplechasers they were training up.

Of course, it couldn't last. The Kingsport Cup wasn't a steeplechase, it was a flat race. Briar's family didn't travel to races; they sold to people who did. People like Adrian Worthington, the man who was bearing down on her right now with all of the warmth and affection of the iceberg that had taken down the Titanic. "Briar," he greeted. "You're ten minutes late."

He was smiling. Of course he was smiling. His smile was just as fake as hers, a mere turning up of the lips just at the ends. His face had probably settled that way; it never changed. He'd worn the same expression when he'd traded her father's debts for her hand in marriage, and he'd worn the same expression when he'd laid down the ground rules for their married life together. He wore it when he negotiated all of his business deals, and when he made the decision to put down an injured horse.

She tilted her head up to receive his perfunctory kiss on the cheek. A few cameras clicked. How had the press gotten back here? "There was an accident on 26. Tractor trailer jackknifed." She lowered her voice and pitched it so that only he could hear. "You're welcome to check if you're concerned."

He rolled his eyes. "I don't care what the excuse was. I just don't like being embarrassed." His lips barely moved; someone watching, even from a few feet away, would never have known that he was speaking. "Don't let it happen again." Adrian pulled back a little, setting up a perfect pose for the cameras to get the happy couple side by side.

Briar smiled for the pictures and tried to tune out the reporters. They weren't interested in her; she didn't need to play more than a passive role in this charade. Race day was Adrian's day to shine. He would talk about the horses he had in the race, and he would talk about how they were trained and bred and housed. He'd talk about his staff, and he'd talk about his own success story. All Briar had to do was smile and look good.

She tried to think about it like she'd have thought about any other job, back when she was in college. She'd waited tables. She'd checked people out at the library. She'd had a couple of modeling jobs, too – nothing big, but a few local jobs here and there. This was no different. If she kept telling herself that, eventually she'd believe it.

She stood there in the barn for an hour and a half, plastic smile frozen to her face while Adrian rumbled on about land and breeding and management. Her feet hurt after twenty minutes; her calves started to cramp up after forty. Platform sandals were stylish, and they made her long legs look even better, but they weren't suitable for stables or for long periods of standing.

Finally, the trumpet blared over the loudspeaker, followed by a garbled announcement that Briar knew meant that it was time to go to work. The main event wasn't for another few hours, but there were plenty of earlier races to keep people's attention – and keep their money flowing into the racetrack's coffers. Adrian would have to focus now, to make sure that everything ran smoothly for every horse he'd brought.

Sometimes Briar resented her status as "the wife." She had a degree in equine management, which was more than at least half of the staff could say. She had plenty of experience on a very successful horse farm. She could have made suggestions that would have saved Adrian thousands, and would have won him more money too.

Then she saw the way he treated his staff, and the resentment bled away. She might be décor, but at least he didn't micromanage her like that.

She strolled away. Maybe things would be less dull in the stands. She did, after all, have a ticket.

She found her way to her assigned seat, crammed between a white guy who might have witnessed Reconstruction and a woman with light brown skin whose hat threatened to eat all of Section Three. Briar made a good faith effort to maintain her position, but after having to spend the entire Breeder's Cup

Challenge race with one hand raised to block the hat's repeated attempts to poke out her eyes, she decided she might do better from inside the grandstand. Adrian might get cranky about the wasted money, but let him; it wasn't like they couldn't afford a box, or like he would put her on staff.

She bought herself a half-wilted salad from the concession stand and sat at a high table, alone, to eat it. She could watch the next Weight for Age run, an Appaloosa-specific half-mile race that some people were trying to talk up as a qualifier for the Jockey Club Gold Cup. Briar didn't know about all that, but she did have a horse in this one herself. Sure, Adrian got all the credit, but Briar's Sweet Rose was Briar's own horse, bred on her father's farm back in Virginia and brought with her into the marriage. Briar had been the one to train that horse, from the moment she'd been old enough to take a rider to the day they'd put her in the trailer to come down here to Tennessee.

Adrian had smirked, calling it a cute hobby.

Briar watched, glued to the screen as her Appaloosa worked. She recognized the jockey: her own stepson, Craig. Craig would do well; he loved Rosie almost as much as Briar did and would take good care of her.

The filly had a strong competitive streak in her, which wasn't unusual for her bloodline. What did stand out was the way that she strove. She strained as she galloped, long neck stretched out in the sun as she raced toward the finish line. Briar held her breath, but she needn't have worried. By the time that Rosie crossed that line, there wasn't another horse within two body lengths of her.

She turned away as they showed a shocked Adrian receiving the prize and the wreath. She didn't care about the accolades or anything like that. It just burned in her gut to see Adrian getting the credit for her hard work. At the same time, he was the one to foot the bill for it all, so technically even if she'd been an employee it would still be him up there.

She forced the smile back onto her face and threw her food away. She didn't get to feel regrets, and she had nothing to regret in the first place. This was a good thing. Rosie had won, and that was what mattered. Rosie had won, and she'd won with Craig riding her.

Done with lunch, and unwilling to return to her seat, Briar considered her options. She could wander the grandstand like a lonely ghost, but that would make her feet hurt and would probably get dull after about ten minutes. She could head to one of the three bars that this racetrack offered. Why this track offered three different bars she had no idea, but they did and they were an option. She didn't want to spend her day sitting in a bar; she could always get Adrian to order a staff member to drive her back to the hotel, but that felt undignified.

The idea of slipping back into the barn area became more and more palatable. She found her feet heading back there before she really knew what she was doing, and she didn't try to stop herself. Given an option, she'd always go for the horses.

No one gave her a hard time when she let herself into the restricted area, not this time around.

She took a quick glimpse into Worthington Stables. Everyone over there was busy; no one even noticed her looking over at them. Craig caught a glimpse, but he didn't have time to do more than wave. He had other races to run. She checked in with the barn assistant responsible for Rosie and made sure that her girl was well taken care of, and then she went for a wander again.

A scream caught her attention. A woman screaming in a place like this wasn't something she heard every day. A lot of people in racing still thought that a woman's place in racing was out in the stands, wearing ridiculous hats, so another feminine presence back here in the barns absolutely caught Briar's attention. The fact that the woman was in distress made her even more concerned.

Briar wasn't the only one concerned, but a couple of well-placed and seemingly accidental elbows brought her to the front of the crowd that had gathered to see whatever spectacle might have cropped up. Briar gasped, hand to her mouth. The scene was grim. A small crowd had gathered in a semi-circle around a stall. Inside the stall, a restive colt had become spooked, and had turned on a jockey. By the time that Briar arrived, the jockey was on the ground, trying to defend her face and head against a rearing colt.

If someone didn't do something, the jockey was going to die. Unfortunately for the jockey, no one seemed to be particularly inclined toward action.

Briar stepped in, palms up and out, and started speaking to the horse. She didn't pay much attention to her words, just to her tone. Within a few seconds, the colt calmed, getting all four feet onto the ground. Briar didn't trust him, of course. She didn't break eye contact. Instead, she reached out and put a hand on the colt's neck. "Can someone get me a lunge? Is there someplace where we can get this guy out on a lunge line?"

She heard people scrambling behind her, but didn't dare look. While the jockey struggled to her feet, a bruise with the distinctive mark of a horseshoe already starting to take shape on her face, other people scurried to Briar's side with a lunge line. "There's a ring right out here, ma'am," said a young man. "Right this way."

Briar heroically refrained from rolling her eyes as she attached the colt to the lunge line, patting and soothing him the whole time. She hadn't had a chance to check his name before she'd gone charging in, but he didn't seem to object to being called Bob, and it gave Briar something to call him for now so she went with it.

The small crowd watched as she led the horse out to the ring, following the barn assistant. He put a lunge whip into her hand, but she didn't think she'd need it. She hadn't needed ten seconds in that stall to realize that Bob wasn't going to benefit from a hard sell approach. He had a lot of pent-up energy, and a lot of nerves. The poor thing probably hadn't gotten nearly enough exercise since he'd gotten to Kingsport. She had half a mind to talk to his trainer.

Half an hour on the lunge line and Bob was giving Briar nuzzles and cuddles. She passed him back to the barn hand with strict instructions to give him a very gentle rubdown and some good oats when the jockey approached. The smaller woman had been watching with a mixture of fear and awe and Briar hadn't been unaware, she just couldn't afford to take the time to think about it. "So what are you, the horse whisperer?" the jockey asked.

"I don't know about all that." Briar blushed. "I know what I'm doing, but I wouldn't go quite that far." She held out a hand. "Briar Sharp."

The jockey took the hand and shook it. "Adrian Worthington's wife. I know who you are. Didn't know you had that kind of talent." She grinned and shook Briar's hand. "Billie West. Thanks for that; we just took delivery of Kelvin today."

Briar relaxed a little. They couldn't have known, she guessed, and at least they weren't planning on racing poor Bob like that. "I think it's going to be a little while before he's ready to race. He's a beautiful horse, though. Magnificent."

"Isn't he? I figured I'd give him a little workout but I guess he wasn't ready for it. Last time we ever go with Shepherd, at least as far as taking his word for it that a horse is 'race-ready.' Good thing Mickey knows better than to take someone's word for that kind of thing anyway."

Briar snorted. "Yeah, good thing. I'd hate to think what would happen." She glanced at Billie. "Are you okay? We should get some ice on that bruise."

Billie waved a hand. "I've had worse. You know how colts can be."

Briar shrugged. "Doesn't mean that you shouldn't get some ice on it."

Billie chuckled. "True."

Briar grinned. "Well, if you all don't have any ice you can come back to our barn, we've got plenty."

"No, no. We've got some around here somewhere, I just –"

Billie cut herself off as a man came barging into the clean stall they were using as an office. The man was tall, way too tall to be a jockey. He wore work clothes, jeans and a plaid shirt, but something about the way that the other workers stood back from him told Briar that this guy wasn't just another barn assistant looking for a chance to make it big doing something else.

He raced to Billie's side, pressing a bag of frozen peas to her bruise. "That colt's going to be a problem, isn't he?" the tall man asked, eyes only for Billie and her injury.

"No, no." Billie waved a hand. "It was just a bad introduction, and then I went in there thinking that he'd be calm. Misunderstandings all around. I won't be getting any dates for the next few days, but I'm okay, Mickey." She smiled. It had to hurt, given the way her face had gotten all banged up, but she did it anyway. "Ms. Sharp, or should I say Mrs. Worthington, was here to keep me safe."

"I go by Sharp." Briar swallowed. She'd made the decision to keep her maiden name when she'd been sent into this marriage, but it had never sounded so rebellious as it did now. "Briar Sharp." She held out a bold hand, surprised at herself.

The stranger rose to his feet. He had to be over six foo two, maybe as much as six foot four. His dark skin was unlined, and he'd cut his still-dark hair close to his head. "Mickey Ratcliff," he said, shaking her hand. "Thank you for your help with Kelvin. He's new to our stable; we're just bringing him home today. I can assure you that you'd never see us putting a horse into a situation that would cause a reaction like that under any other circumstances."

Briar smiled at him. She knew the name, of course. Who didn't? He'd become an overnight success, a billionaire by thirty just on his horse sense and his racing know-how. "Just back from Dubai, if I'm not mistaken."

He grinned. He hadn't let go of her hand yet, and Briar had to admit that she didn't want him to. "You know the business pretty well."

She raised an eyebrow. "Shouldn't I? I mean, it's in my best interests, right?" She squeezed his hand, just a little.

"Of course." He blinked. "Of course. I mean, yes, of course. That would be important to you. Your husband's business, of course."

Billie popped up from behind Mickey. Briar had all but forgotten that the jockey was there. "She's got more know-how than just that, Mick. Come on."

Briar shook her head. "I majored in equine management at college, but that was a long time ago."

Mickey snickered. "Not that long ago." He checked his watch. "The big race is about to start."

Chapter 2

Billie looked at Briar. "I'm sure you'll want to watch from Mr. Worthington's box."

Briar shook her head. "He doesn't take a box at races like this. He prefers a more hands-on approach to management." She forced her face back into blandness, lest her words be construed as an insult or a shot at Adrian. "He's spent a lot of time building up his stables; he's passionate about how every detail is executed."

Mickey glanced over in the direction of Adrian's horses. Briar followed his gaze, only to see Adrian haranguing a stable assistant about the lead he was using for Bitter Banter, the horse that had just taken second in the Silver Cup. On the one hand, Briar agreed with her husband; even at this distance she could see that they were using a lead that never worked well on the colt. On the other hand, not a lot of people responded well to that sort of treatment, either. The poor assistant's face had gone red, then white, and Briar wouldn't be surprised to learn that the young man had turned in his notice tomorrow.

"I can see that," Mickey drawled, raising an eyebrow. "So where are you supposed to sit to watch the race, a hay bale?"

Briar laughed. "I wouldn't mind, if I had dressed a little differently. No, he got me a ticket in the stands."

Mickey made a face. "Oh come on. I mean, Ms. Sharp, I would be delighted if you would do me the honor of joining me in my private box to enjoy the upcoming race." He held out an arm.

Briar glanced back at Adrian. Her husband had turned back to his work and was now taking out his frustrations on one of the junior trainers. "I would be delighted," she told Mickey, accepting his arm.

Mickey turned to Billie. "Billie, I trust you. Get it done, okay?"

Billie winked at him. "I got your back, big guy." With that, the tiny woman disappeared into the flurry of people preparing for the race, and Briar walked out of the stable on the arm of someone who could be described as her husband's biggest rival.

The crowd of photographers and journalists, who had been hanging around the barn entrance like flies in the barn itself, took notice. Out in the regular world, Briar certainly didn't count as a celebrity. She could go to the mall without causing a fuss; she could go to the grocery store in peace, if she ever found a need to go to the grocery store at all. In the racing world, Adrian Worthington was a legend, and his wife was by necessity part of his aura of glamour.

In fact, that was the whole reason Adrian had wanted a wife in the first place.

So while Briar might be able to run errands or go to the doctor without any hassle from paparazzi, once she got onto a racetrack things changed. "Hey, Prosperina," called one of the reporters. "Whatcha doing with Ratcliff? Does Pluto know you're stepping out on him?"

The men, unshaven and in rumpled, cheap suits, gave dirty little laughs. Inside, Briar quailed at their accusation. She wasn't a cheater, but she'd seen all too often what could happen to a good woman in the face of filthy accusations. It didn't help that Mickey was tall, and handsome, and half Adrian's age.

She couldn't let any of that show, though. She just pasted her most vapid smile across her face, straightened her back and kept her head high. That had been something that Adrian had warned her about, early in their relationship. *Never let them see you hurt. They'll hurl the most vile things at you that they can, because you are a woman, and you are a Black woman,*

and because you are my wife. Don't acknowledge them.
Don't speak to them. Just pretend that they aren't there. It's
what I've always done and it's what Marilee, my late wife, did
too.

Mickey, though, paused to speak with them. "Oh come on, boys. Do you really think that there is some kind of foolish rivalry between Adrian Worthington and me? Come on, be real. I'm barely getting back into the U. S. racing circuit. Mr. Worthington is more of a teacher or a mentor. And as such, there is absolutely nothing improper about giving his lovely wife a comfortable place to sit during the race. You all know where it is, and I'm sure you'll be watching us the whole time." He winked at them. "Honest, there is no funny business going on here; it would be like shooting myself in the foot." He kept walking toward the exit at the same pace they'd been moving before the dirty-minded reporters interrupted them.

The journalists gaped after them, too stunned to write or take photos.

"That was amazing!" Briar murmured, keeping her face as stiff as she could. Once they were in the corridor that led to the private boxes she could let her guard down a little bit, but not much. "You shut them right up!"

"I'm not exactly new at this," he pointed out with a wry grin. "Some of the places I've been racing have had press that make those guys look like they're throwing softballs. It helps to talk to them, though. Let them think that you have some kind of relationship with them; then they treat you much more kindly when they do have something to report." Now his grin turned wicked. "Prosperina and Pluto?"

"Ugh." She clutched at her stomach. "They came up with that one when our wedding was announced. Some hack thought he'd get some use out of his degree in classics and here we are."

An usher let them into the luxury box as Mickey nodded a few times in acknowledgment. "Well, I suppose it's important to encourage people to study those fields, you know. We shouldn't be too hard on him."

Briar threw her head back and laughed. "I probably never would have thought about it like that. I wonder if he wrote his first draft in Latin?"

"He might have. Can I get you anything? A cocktail, something to eat?"

She shook her head. "Water is fine for me, or maybe coffee. I still need to drive back to the hotel."

"Oh? Where are you staying?"

"I'm at the Hilton in Kingsport." She glanced toward the track.

"What a coincidence! I'm at the Hilton myself."

She turned to face him. "For real? You're not bunking down here with your horses?"

He turned away from the tablet, where he was ordering their drinks. "For real. I trust my staff, Ms. Sharp."

"Briar, please."

He smiled and ducked his head, cheeks glowing. "Briar. I trust my staff. I'm confident that I've made good hiring decisions and that my trainers are all perfectly capable of keeping my horses safe. I've spent a lot of years sleeping in stables; I don't have to do that anymore. Billie's staying at the Hilton, too. She stayed on-site before the race, but she wants a real bed and a nice, hot shower after racing all day."

Briar smiled politely. What was the relationship between Mickey and Billie, anyway? They'd seemed oddly familiar, for an employer and employee. "So I assume that you've got a

horse in this run." She racked her brain to make the

connection. "Purple Reins."

Mickey's laugh echoed through the box. "You do follow the

field pretty closely. I'm surprised you're not more involved

with the management of your husband's stables."

She blushed and looked out over the track again. None of the

horses were lined up. "I guess he wasn't looking for a

business partner."

"Hm. I suppose not. It's a shame. I saw you with Kelvin

downstairs and you certainly know what you're doing. You

truly love horses. If I ask you a question, will I get an honest

answer?"

Briar bit her lip. "Maybe."

"Briar's Sweet Rose, who won the Weight by Year earlier. Is she actually yours, or is that just a clever name?" Mickey leaned in and rested his chin on one hand.

Briar blushed and looked away. "I don't hold the title or anything, but I trained her. I bred her, back before we got married. She comes from my father's farm."

"She's one impressive filly. Are you thinking of breeding her?"

Briar sighed. "That's not really my decision to make. I do think that she comes from good stock, but I'm not sure that Adrian wants to explore those lines. He's more interested in thoroughbreds right now." That wasn't giving away trade secrets at all; Adrian had said as much in the papers. Mickey could have learned as much by picking up one of the racing broadsides and reading it over his morning coffee.

The fact that she'd said it to someone just because he'd asked, because he was the first person to ask her opinion in years, shouldn't make her feel guilty at all.

Now the horses were being brought out. She picked out Martin's Hundred, the horse Adrian had in today's race, and she folded her lips against a comment. How could Adrian have sent this horse out here with a limp like that? It wasn't a huge limp, he wasn't lame or hurt, but something was clearly bothering the poor thing and there was no way he was going to perform. Craig would do his best, but there was only so much he'd be able to do with material like that.

By contrast, Purple Reins looked ready and rested as he trotted out to his starting position. Billie, too, looked perfectly composed and ready to get to work. There was no way that Mickey's horse was going to lose the main event.

The waiter arrived with their coffees and disappeared again. Briar lifted hers to Mickey in a kind of salute. "Well," she said, taking a deep breath before sipping her drink. "Here goes."

"I take it you saw what I saw?"

Briar liked Mickey. She liked him more than she should, to be honest, but she couldn't slam Adrian to his rival. "Maybe he picked something up in his shoe on his way out to the track. Craig's a fine jockey; he'll be able to handle it."

As it turned out, Craig and Martin's Hundred did much better than Briar thought that they would have considering the way Martin's Hundred was walking. They came in third. Purple Reins came in first, and Briar couldn't find it in her heart to feel bad about it.

"You should get down there to accept your trophy," she told Mickey. "Thank you for the company, and for the loan of your box seat."

"No, thank you, Briar." He took her hand and held it for a moment. "I hope we'll meet up again."

Briar blushed. She might hope so too, but she knew they wouldn't. For now, Mickey had to go and accept his triumph, and Briar had to go and try to deflect whatever fallout might arise from the disaster of a third place finish.

By the time that she got down to the Worthington Stables section of the barn, Adrian was already in fine form. Craig stood before him, helmet off and head bowed. Briar could see the tears in the younger man's eyes as his father lit into him before the entire stable.

"How could you let this happen?" Adrian bellowed, slamming a stack of papers down onto a hay bale so hard that a few horses whinnied. "Honestly, how stupid can you be? We had this in the bag! Martin's Hundred is an experienced racer, but you somehow managed to bungle the race."

Craig said nothing, just kept his head bowed. Briar rushed to the scene. Martin's Hundred, the horse in question, seemed to have some kind of sense that the situation wasn't good. He'd pressed his entire body against the wall of his stall and watched the scene unfold with wide eyes.

Briar knew better than to say anything. Early in the marriage, she'd tried to intervene on Craig's behalf, only to have Adrian get even angrier at Craig that a woman younger than Craig saw fit to spring to his defense for things that she couldn't hope to know anything about. Instead, she slipped into the stall with Martin's Hundred and picked up the hoof on the leg that had looked off to her. Sure enough, something had gotten wedged into the thoroughbred's shoe, badly enough to cause a break in his gait but not enough to make him come up lame.

Briar reached out, without a word, to the nearest barn assistant. He passed her a tool, and she popped the offending item out without a problem. Martin's Hundred whinnied and gave her a little nuzzle, and she patted the poor horse on the neck and let him lean into her in return. The poor horse must have been terrified, must still be terrified.

She held up the tool and the intrusive piece of debris as stable hands, trainers, her husband and her stepson stared. Craig fought a little grin.

Adrian took the items from her, going from screaming mad to cold apathy in a second. "This is what made him lose the race?"

"Yes." She looked down for a moment, and then she remembered that she had nothing to be ashamed of. "I noticed that he looked a little off, in his gait, while I was watching the race." She indicated the debris with her eyes. "It looks like a bit of concrete from the stable floor."

Her meaning, subtly expressed, was clear. Adrian had inspected Martin's Hundred before letting him go out onto the track.

"Hm." Adrian's lip curled. "And you noticed this from Mickey Ratcliff's luxury box, I suppose?"

Her heart froze inside her chest, but she had nothing to be ashamed of, nothing to fear. It wasn't as though there hadn't been six paparazzi sitting there taking pictures the whole time, proving that she had nothing to fear. "Yes. He made the offer and I accepted, and it's a good thing I did. I wonder if the hitch in his gait would have been noticeable up close." She smiled at him, vapid and bland, and shrugged. "Anyway, all's well that ends well. Martin's Hundred is healthy, and considering what was going on with the poor thing we're lucky he finished third." She didn't dare reach out and touch Craig's shoulder, but she could meet his eyes and trust that he'd understand what she meant.

Adrian glared, but then he rolled his neck. "I suppose there's nothing to do about it now. All right. Let's get him cleaned up. Tomorrow we've got the Kingston Horse Show, let's turn in early and make sure we're ready to meet all those aficionados." He turned to his wife and son. "Craig, why don't you drive your mother back to the hotel? You don't have to stay on-site tonight. You won't be needed tomorrow."

Craig's hands clenched into fists at his side, but he just nodded and grabbed a duffel out of one of the stalls with the cots. "You ready, Mama?" he asked Briar, in a voice that was a little more like a growl than anything else.

Briar nodded, and led her stepson out to the car. He tossed his duffel into the trunk and got into the passenger seat. They both relaxed once the doors were closed and the windows up; maybe this was a little outside of Adrian's strict instructions but there was no way that she was going to ask Craig to drive after he'd jockeyed for two races and endured a dressing-down by his father.

She called the hotel and asked for a second room to be charged to her account, which they were more than willing to accommodate. After that, the pair settled into a companionable silence for about twenty minutes. Then, Craig spoke. "You could really see the thing with his hoof from way up there with Mickey Ratcliff?"

"You bet." She kept her eyes on the road.

"Damn it. I told him something didn't feel right." He turned his head away.

Briar didn't say anything. She couldn't. She didn't have any words to offer him.

They got to the hotel and checked Craig in. It was still early enough that Briar couldn't help but feel a bit of a pang at the early night, but she'd survive. She had a few books she wanted to read, anyway. She'd just settled in with the first chapter of a new mystery when someone knocked at her door.

Standing there, just outside her door, were Billie and Mickey. "Since you're staying in the same hotel as we are," Mickey began, "and since we're all getting along so swimmingly, I wondered if you might want to grab a bite to eat and maybe a couple of drinks down at the hotel bar." He gestured to Billie. "All three of us. No funny business."

Briar grinned. Adrian would be upset, but he wasn't here. And he hadn't outright forbidden her to associate with Mickey. She just needed some way to stop tongues from wagging. "Do you mind if I bring my stepson, Craig? He's had a rough day and he could use a little R&R as much as anyone."

Billie glanced to the door next to Briar's room. "Craig Worthington, the jockey?" She grinned a little, almost like a cat. "Oh, sure. I have no problem with that at all."

They collected Craig, who had already showered and changed out of his jockey uniform and into street clothes. Then they descended to the hotel restaurant and bar, where Craig ordered a gin and tonic and turned to Billie. "Before any drinking starts," he said, "I want to say that you were incredible out there. A hundred percent, you deserved that win. I've never seen a jockey quite so composed out there, and what the hell happened to your face?"

Billie and Mickey laughed while Briar blushed. "Didn't Briar tell you?" Billie put a hand on Briar's arm and recounted the story of how they'd met. Briar tried to downplay it, but Mickey wouldn't hear of it. "I think we'd have lost our best jockey, and I'd have lost my best friend, if Briar hadn't come along."

"Yeah, well, Briar definitely knows her way around a stable. And around a horse." Craig raised a glass to Briar. "Can't say as I'm surprised. So tell me, you all just got back from Dubai, right?"

Mickey nodded and started telling a story about the Meydan Racecourse and how he'd won his first Dubai World Cup, which turned out to be a much more entertaining story than Briar would have thought it could have been. Billie followed it up with a story about a race she and Mickey had won in South Korea that was less interesting because of the race than because of the trouble that they'd gotten themselves into, and subsequently out of.

Craig then followed with his own funny stories, and even Briar managed to dredge up a few knee-slappers that didn't make Adrian look bad. She soon lost track of time, not because she was drinking but because she was having so much fun.

It had been a long time since she'd just let loose and laughed like this, just sat back and relaxed and had a conversation with friends. Craig did his best, but he was just one man and Adrian preferred that his wife spend her time in more "mature" company. Billie might be a year or two older than Briar, and she knew for a fact that Mickey was thirty just like Craig. All four of them shared the same pop culture references, they all knew the same songs, and they all had watched the same shows.

All of that was a balm for Briar's wounded soul. She hadn't realized just how much she missed youthful company until she had it again, until she didn't have to sit and be prim and proper and silent and doll-like. It felt good, and she never wanted it to stop.

The question was, how much of what she was feeling was from the joy of being around people like herself again and how much was from being around Mickey, specifically?

Mickey didn't do anything that she could single out as flirtatious. He was attentive, of course, but that seemed to be normal for him. He was attentive to Billie, and he'd made it abundantly clear throughout the evening that he was not interested in Billie. He was attentive to Craig, too, for that matter. But something about the self-made billionaire called out to Briar. It wasn't just the shared experiences, or the shared love of horses. Something passed between them every time their arms brushed against one another, or every time their eyes met across the table.

Mickey asked her for her phone number when he escorted her back up to her room at the end of the night. She should say no; it wasn't right, exchanging phone numbers with another man when she was a married woman. He might mean nothing by it, but she knew her own heart and she knew that it wasn't pure.

She didn't raise any objections when Craig gave both of their numbers to both Mickey and Billie, catching Briar's eye and winking. Oh, this was going to end badly, but it felt so good right now.

Chapter 3

Briar slept alone. This wasn't unusual for her; she'd slept alone every night since her wedding. She'd been glad to sleep alone, too, when she considered the alternative. That night, after having dinner with Mickey Ratcliff, was the first night that she dreamed about sleeping next to someone else.

Oh, sure. She'd had dreams about "someone." She hadn't exactly lived in a convent when she'd been away at college, and there were plenty of men who caught her eye. Once she'd become a negotiating tool, a piece of chattel for two men to exchange between them, she'd refused to let her mind go there – at all, ever, not even while she was sleeping. She could never let herself dream of someone specific, someone with a face, for fear that she'd slip up in the waking world and put her whole family at risk.

It had been wrong for her father to trade her away in exchange for money like that, sure. At the same time, she didn't know what else he was supposed to have done, when Adrian Worthington had offered him financial support in exchange for his daughter's hand in marriage.

So Briar couldn't let herself think about anyone, at all. Her dreams had all been populated by men whose faces were hidden by shadows, and in the waking world she stayed very carefully in her place. In return, her father got to keep the farm. Her mother got the medical treatment she needed for her severe rheumatoid arthritis. Her sisters got to go to school. It wasn't a bad trade-off, or so she told herself.

Until that night, after the Kingston Cup. That night, she lay in the hotel bed alone, and she dreamed of Mickey.

She dreamed of those big, strong hands on her body, warming skin that had been left cold for far too long. She dreamed of his dark lips on her flesh, seeking out all of the places that could make her moan. She dreamed of his body covering hers, penetrating deep inside her and filling that place that had been empty for four long years. She dreamed that he held her afterward, wrapped around her body like he could shelter her from every bad thing in the world.

When she woke up she almost cried. She hadn't done that since the morning before her wedding.

She'd slipped up somehow, let the cast-iron discipline of her mind and heart slip. She couldn't think about any man, much less Mickey Ratcliff. While Mickey might say nice things about Adrian to the press, Briar knew how Adrian felt about the young and talented horseman. Mickey's fast path to wealth and fame had eclipsed Adrian's own rags-to-riches success story, and Adrian's ego was threatened by it.

She went to take a shower, and hopefully to wash some of the distraction from her mind. When she emerged, she found a new message waiting on her phone from Craig. He and Billie wanted to go see the Netherland Inn and Complex, a local historic house museum dating back to the early nineteenth century. Mickey was going to join them; did Briar want to come along too?

Briar knew that she should stay behind. She should be a good wife and stay in the hotel. Maybe she could go so far as to get her nails done. When her phone buzzed again, giving her a message from Mickey reiterating the message, her resistance crumbled.

After all, what could be the harm of a day out among friends? That was all. And Craig would be there. Nothing could happen if her stepson was there to act as a chaperone, for crying out loud.

She texted them both back, telling them that she would join them. Then she got dressed.

They got breakfast first, enjoying a quick meal at a small diner that claimed to have the best waffles in Tennessee. As it turned out, they weren't lying. Once they'd finished their breakfast, they got up and went to visit the old hotel.

Briar didn't care much about the old hotel. She did care about the company. The quartet wandered the house and grounds in high spirits, and none seemed to be in higher spirits than Craig and Billie. "There seems to be a lot of chemistry between those two," Mickey said, standing just close enough that she could feel his body heat as they watched the two jockeys examine the stable.

"There does. I'm sure they'll have plenty of chances to see one another; they'll be riding in all of the same races." She blushed, but didn't move away. She liked how perfectly she fit into this man's body.

"And how do you think Mr. Worthington will feel about that?" He raised an eyebrow, watching as Billie threw her head back and laughed.

"He'll be upset. Not because he'd have a problem with Billie, although he's not a huge fan of women being too involved with the sport. My husband's a very competitive man."

"I'm sure he must be." Mickey smirked, just a little. "You and Craig get along very well."

"We do. He's been very kind." She looked up to see that Craig and Billie were on their way back to where Briar and Mickey were watching and breathed a little easier. She shouldn't let herself open up like that. She shouldn't let herself get attached.

After they'd finished with the Netherland Inn, they decided to find lunch and then go for a few rounds of mini-golf. Briar hadn't done mini-golf since she'd been a kid, but she was having enough fun that she decided she was game. Besides, nothing was less sexy or endearing than mini-golf, or so she thought.

She thought wrong. The quartet stood out in the warm springtime sun, laughing so hard at one another's jokes and mistakes that two different middle-aged men came up and asked them to "tone it down, for crying out loud, this is a family establishment!" That only made them laugh even harder.

The fun continued into dinner. Briar couldn't have said where they ate or what they had. All that she could say for certain was that she had a hard time turning away from the hearts in Craig's eyes every time he looked at Billie. She'd always wanted someone to look at her like that. She'd thought, when she'd married Adrian, that she was giving up any hope of anything of the sort.

Now she sat there next to Mickey, and she couldn't deny that there wasn't a lot of difference between the way that Mickey was looking at her and the way Craig looked at Billie. She felt like the most precious gem in a crown when he turned his beautiful brown eyes on her like that. The only problem was that they couldn't act on it.

They talked a lot during dinner, and over drinks back at the hotel afterward. Billie told them about growing up in Washington, D.C., and how she'd gotten into a lot of trouble at a very young age. Someone had gotten her into a program that put "troubled youth" into horseback riding lessons, and she'd been hooked. The owner of the stable where she'd been taking lessons had seen her talent, and had taken a chance on her.

That stable owner had been Mickey's foster parent, number ten in what had felt like an endless succession to the young boy. He'd turned out to be the last foster parent in the line, though. He'd recognized a talent in Mickey, too, and he'd encouraged him. "If it weren't for old Mr. Ratcliff, I wouldn't be where I am today." Mickey gave a little smile. "It wasn't easy, don't get me wrong. Old man Ratcliff wasn't exactly the affectionate type."

"No, he wasn't." Billie agreed with a laugh.

"But he gave me three things. He gave me a trade, one that a throwaway country kid that no one wanted could take anywhere in the world and build a life for himself with. He gave me hope, that there was a future for me. And he gave me Billie." Mickey winked at his friend. "I met Billie there, we got to be best friends, and neither one of us has looked back. That's why I took his name, when I aged out of the foster system."

Briar raised her glass. "To Old Man Ratcliff, then."

The others all joined in her toast. "To Old Man Ratcliff." The glasses clinked, like small bells pealing against the background noise of the hotel bar, and Briar relaxed against her chair back. She couldn't be unconscious of Mickey's arm, slung casually over the back of the chair like it belonged there. She wanted it to belong there. She wanted it around her shoulders, or her waist.

Maybe coming out tonight was a bad idea after all.

After they'd finished their drinks, Billie and Craig disappeared toward their rooms. Briar hid a smirk with one hand. "What do you think the odds are that they'll stay in separate rooms?"

"Now that's a bet I'm not about to take." Mickey chuckled. "That's good, though. They deserve to be happy."

She looked up at him. "It can't last. His father would lose his mind."

Mickey moved his arm. Briar found that his hand was covering hers, warm and sheltering hers. "His father have some kind of problem with love?"

She should pull away, but she didn't. She just looked up at him. "It's not like they compete with one another or anything."

He snorted. "I think that would just be part of the appeal, don't you? All that adrenaline on the track just pushing them further off of it." He grinned, dirty and wicked. "But then again, maybe it would just make them even more tender after a race."

She wished she'd worn something lighter; somehow her clothes seemed too warm. She knew he wasn't really talking about Billie and Craig anymore. "You don't honestly think it would go like that. His father would never —"

"Give up that kind of control?" When Briar gasped, Mickey shook his head. "Come on. Do you think there's anyone who doesn't know that he chose Craig's last three girlfriends for him? How he expected those relationships to last, I have no idea."

Briar looked away. "It's not my place to get involved with their relationship."

"But you must have an opinion." Mickey grinned.

"But that opinion doesn't matter," she countered. "It wouldn't improve things for Craig, and Craig does stick around and tolerate it."

"True." He stood up. "And so do you."

Briar shook her head. "That's neither here nor there." She rose too. The rest of the bar faded away. "I should get back to my room."

"Yeah." He closed his eyes for a moment and breathed out, slow and deep. "Yeah, that's a good idea. Good night, Briar." He kissed her cheek, lips feeling like little jolts of electricity on her skin before she made her escape.

Once she made it back to her room, she took off a couple of layers of clothing and collapsed against a wall. She should take a cold shower, or maybe run down the hall and fill up the ice bucket. She'd never been so affected by a man before. Had she gotten this pathetic since she'd gotten married, that a little bit of flirtatious attention from a man was enough to get her all riled up?

Or maybe it was just Mickey?

Mickey was an impressive man, that much was certain. He was handsome, but his appeal went beyond mere looks. He was strong. He'd overcome great odds to get to where he was. Some of it was luck – he'd been incredibly lucky to have someone recognize his talent and be in a position to nurture it - but he's also made opportunities for himself.

And once he'd started making a name for himself, he hadn't turned into a robot, or whatever it was that Adrian had become. Mickey was warm, and generous. He was friendly and he didn't seem compelled to micromanage everything in his orbit. Mickey was, genuinely, a good guy.

Of course, none of that had much bearing on the way her body felt about him. Maybe her heart and her mind could appreciate the way his workers all seemed happy, or the way he treated everyone around him with respect, but her body was drawn to that smile, those hands, and that mouth. When had she last wanted a man like this? She couldn't remember. She didn't know; she didn't want to think about it. If she thought about it, she'd have to acknowledge that she wasn't as okay with the past four years as she'd pretended to be.

Someone knocked on the door.

She didn't have to look to know who it was. She threw a bathrobe over herself and stuck her head out the door. "Mickey, what's wrong?" she asked him. He shouldn't be here. She shouldn't let him see her like this, even though she still had plenty of clothes on under the robe.

"I couldn't stand being without you," Mickey whispered. "Let me in, Briar. Please." He looked down into her eyes, with so much passion and meaning, that she couldn't help but step aside and open the door.

He slipped inside, and she closed and locked the door behind him. "Mickey, we shouldn't. My husband – I'm married."

He put his hands on her shoulders. "You don't want him. He barely knows you're alive." He ducked his head down and claimed her mouth.

Even years ago, when Briar had been free and in college, she'd never been kissed like this. Mickey kissed like he could coax her soul right out of her body. Maybe he could, if he could convince her to share her body with a man who wasn't her husband.

He pulled up from her mouth with a groan. "Briar," he hissed. "The things you do to me."

"Mickey," she whispered, and kissed him back. She let her robe fall open. If such a little thing as a kiss could heat her body like that, what would the touch of his hands do?

Mickey pulled the robe off of her, leaving her in just her camisole and underwear. She didn't care; she was too busy tugging his polo shirt over his head. His torso made her eyes light up when she saw it; how a busy man like Mickey could make time to develop a body like this completely boggled her mind. As she ran her fingertips over his hard, solid muscles, she smiled. This wasn't the body of some gym rat. Mickey

had gotten his body through hard, physical labor, lifting hay

bales and working his own horses.

He hissed as she dragged the pads of her fingers across his

nipples, a wide smile splitting his face. "That's nice, baby," he

told her, keeping his voice low. "That's real nice."

She looked up into his eyes. How was she supposed to

proceed? It had been so long. Mickey didn't seem to be

bothered by her lack of confidence, though. He kissed her

again, and then he moved his mouth down her jaw, down her

neck, down her collarbone, down her sternum. Even through

the satin of her camisole, that felt good and when he peeled

the flimsy garment off and over her head she didn't fight him.

She leaned up against the wall as he bent down to lick gently

at her right breast. "Yeah," she sighed. "Just like that.

Please, Mickey." Oh, it felt good to have his mouth on her,

she couldn't deny that. After a few seconds of licking he latched right on to her breast, applying just enough suction to make her groan as his huge, callused hands explored every inch of her exposed skin.

When he slipped his fingers beneath the waistband of her panties she didn't object. "This okay?" he asked her, fingers moving just outside that spot she wanted him to touch so badly.

"Please," she said again. "Yes, it's okay. Please."

He grinned and moved his fingers over her wet pussy before stroking once, just lightly, over her clit. She hissed, biting down on her lip. She couldn't afford to get too loud; they didn't need to attract attention.

He knew what she meant, though, and he gave an evil little chuckle. "Oh, baby." His fingers built up pressure and speed as sweat broke out over her entire body. "Yeah, I like to see you just like that. Come on baby. Come for me, Briar. Come nice and hard."

It didn't take long, not with how long she'd gone without. She buried her face in his arm and moaned out her orgasm, even as he kept her going through the aftershocks. Then, he picked her up off of her shaky legs and carried her over to the bed. She could feel his hard manhood pressing into her leg as he carried her, and she looked up at him. "I can..."

"I want to be inside you, Briar. Can I? I mean, will you let me?" He met her eyes and licked his lips.

"Do you have a condom?" She wanted nothing more than to have him inside her, to be joined to him in the most intimate of ways. She was not, however, a fool. She wasn't on the pill, she didn't have an IUD; she hadn't needed anything like that in years.

"Hell yeah." He reached into his wallet and pulled out a little packet.

"Then yes. Please, yes. I need you inside me. Need you inside me like I need air, Mickey." She should blush to talk like that, and maybe she would – later.

Mickey got rid of his pants and boxers in record time, and helped her off with her sodden panties at the same time. Then, he rolled the condom onto himself, lined himself up and sank into Briar.

She cried out when he first entered her. Mickey was a big guy, and her body wasn't used to stretching like that for someone. It didn't exactly hurt; it was just different from what she was used to these days. She adjusted quickly, though. Her body had wanted to be filled up for a while, and her heart wanted this. Wanted Mickey.

She bucked her hips, meeting Mickey thrust for thrust, and he laughed out loud with joy. "Oh, you feel so good, baby. Briar, you can't even understand how good you feel around me."

She wrapped her legs around his waist, fully encircling him and driving him deeper into herself. She couldn't speak, couldn't even form coherent thoughts. All she could do was to hold on and keep him in her for as long as she could.

He picked up the pace and that was it for the dirty talk. The hotel room fell away, taking everything else with it: Adrian, her father, the race, Craig and Billie. There was nothing but Mickey. She wanted nothing but Mickey.

She could tell when he got close, the sweat dripping from his forehead. He slipped a hand between them and worked her clit until she came again, only managing to hide her screams by grabbing a pillow and screaming into it. Mickey collapsed down onto her, and they lay together for a moment as he softened. Then he pulled out of her and went to dispose of the condom.

After, he came back and held her in the bed. "That was amazing," she told him, kissing his lips. "I can't remember the last time I came like that."

"I'm glad you enjoyed." He wrapped a strong arm around her narrow waist. "It was incredible for me, too, you know? You're incredible, Briar. You're just amazing." He kissed her just behind her ear.

They fell asleep like that, with Briar sheltered in the long, strong lines of Mickey's body. She dreamed again, and this time she knew that she was so far over the line as to be lost. She dreamed of waking up in Mickey's arms over and over again, of seeing his beautiful smile every day. She dreamed that she could have days like she'd had today on a regular basis, surrounded by friends instead of by her husband's flunkies.

These were dreams, and they couldn't ever be a reality. She'd been stupid to give herself a night like tonight. Even though the odds of Adrian finding out that she'd slept with Mickey were minimal, letting herself sleep with him had still set herself up for a hard time going forward.

She was still going to have to go back to that cold house in Middleburg. She was still going to have to go back to a life that was essentially without touch, and on the rare occasions that Adrian put his hand on her arm for show, she was going to want to bathe in bleach. The one night together hadn't been the worst part of the affair. The worst had been the day, letting her experience affection and joy on a platonic scale.

There was nothing Briar could do about it now, though. She had made her bed. She might as well enjoy it before she started to miss it.

Chapter 4

Briar woke up the next morning when her phone rang. She thought her heart might stop right then and there. In some ways, that might have been more convenient. It would certainly have hurt less. She reached out and grabbed it off the nightstand. "Hello?" she said.

Adrian's voice came back to her through the speaker, somehow managing to lower the temperature in the room even though he was ten miles away. "Briar," her husband said. "Are you still in bed?"

She blinked and flopped back down onto the pillow. Beside her, Mickey froze. He knew that if he moved an inch he'd risk blowing their cover. "Well, yes, Adrian. I'm still in bed. It's only nine o'clock in the morning."

Adrian harrumphed. Briar could read a lot in his harrumph. "Well. I'm not paying for an extra night in that hotel. You and that no-good son of mine can get yourselves back on home."

"I'll pass the message on. See you soon." Briar waited for the telltale click from Adrian's end before she hung up the phone. "That was Adrian. I need to go." She sent a text to Craig's phone and hoped like hell that her stepson had his turned on.

Mickey sighed. "I guess it was too much to hope for another day." He sat up. "Thank you so much for last night, Briar. I don't think you'll ever know how much that meant to me."

She looked down and away. "I had a good time too. But Mickey – we can't do that again."

"You don't love him."

She forced a little laugh. "That's got nothing to do with it, Mickey. There's stuff going on, stuff you don't know about –"

"So tell me."

She took a deep breath. What would be the harm? "My father got into a bad business deal. A really bad one, with Adrian. Owed him a ton of money and the farm. Adrian said that he would forgive the debt if I married him, and give him an additional hundred grand. Thing is, he didn't actually forgive the debt. He just set it aside."

"So if you try to leave, he's got your family hostage."

"Bingo." She shook her head. "Even last night was a stupid risk I should never have taken." She glanced back at him and felt like her heart was tearing in two. "Even though I can't remember feeling that good in the past, I don't know, eight years?"

Mickey took her hand. "I respect your decision, but you have to know, Briar. I just bought a house not too far from you. We'll be seeing one another from time to time; we won't be able to help it. I'm not going to say or do anything to put you or your family at risk, but it's not like we'll never see one another again."

Oh Lord. She was going to have to see Mickey, be around that meltingly beautiful smile, and not be able to do anything about it. "Okay. Well. I mean that'll be hard." She smiled, maybe a little sadly, and stroked his face. "I'm sorry."

"I'm not." He kissed her before he got out of the bed and searched for his clothes. "I don't regret a thing. Look. If you ever need anything, you can always come to me, okay? Anything at all. I mean it, Briar." He pulled his clothes on as he spoke.

"I know. Thank you again." She squeezed his hand as he slipped out the door.

She took a shower and scrubbed as hard as she could. Logically, she knew that she would look no different when she left the room than she had when she went into it, but she couldn't shake herself free of the notion that somehow her sin would be tattooed on her forehead for all to see.

It didn't matter that her marriage was a sham, something that Adrian needed to complete the image he wanted to sell to the world. It didn't matter that he'd never deigned to touch her, not even on their wedding night, and it didn't matter that the thought of Adrian touching her made her nauseous even before she'd known that Mickey Ratcliff was on the same continent. The fact was, Briar had broken her marriage vows. She had lain with another man, and she knew it.

By the time that she was done washing up and dressed, Craig was ready to go. He took in the state of her hotel room and raised his eyebrow. "You and Mickey, huh?" He grinned. "Well good for you. Lord knows you deserve something in your life."

She wanted to bury her face in her hands, or maybe in the dirt outside. "Craig! How could I be so stupid! What if your father finds out?"

Craig snorted. "He's not going to. I'm going to make sure of it. But Briar – this isn't a bad thing."

"It's awful." She sat down on one of the chairs leading into the hallway. "I shouldn't have done it. It's too much of a risk, too dangerous. What if he goes after my father?"

"My father doesn't give a rat's behind about anything but money, Briar." Craig shook his hand, mouth settling into a bitter little line. "You know it, and I know it. He'll settle for control, but he prefers money. Right now he'll be too busy thinking about the returns from this weekend to even realize that you're in the building." He grinned. "You should see him again."

Briar shook her head. "No way. I can't let that happen. He's too... Mickey's too much. I can't let myself be weak that way. It's too dangerous. I knew what I was getting into when I married Adrian." She sighed and grabbed her suitcase. "Are you ready to go?"

The pair checked out of the hotel and settled in for the long drive back to Middleburg. Ordinarily Briar liked these drives, half the reason she didn't fly or make the drive with Adrian, but today she couldn't help but feel melancholy about the whole thing. Even though she knew that Mickey was going to the same place, the feeling that something was being left behind in Kingsport just wouldn't leave her.

Adrian greeted her with a thin smile when she returned and a few perfunctory questions. Then he returned to his office, and she made the rounds of the stables and grounds. They didn't see each other again for the rest of the day.

She tossed and turned that night, and the next night, and the night after that. Somehow it seemed that now that her body had enjoyed that one night of perfect happiness, it was staging a full on mutiny at the thought of going back to long, cold nights alone. She just couldn't sleep.

She couldn't sleep, but by the end of the first week it was all that she wanted to do. Fatigue made her jittery. It made her dull, too. She sat in near silence at breakfast, sucking down coffee and hoping that it would get her through the day. Sometimes a little extra exercise would help, but other times she found that her own exhaustion made her unsafe around all but the most docile horses.

Mickey called twice. She smiled, in the privacy of her own room, but she didn't call him back. She didn't even listen to the messages. She couldn't afford to. If she were already dealing with insomnia from one night together, how much worse would it be if she let herself listen to his voice?

Craig continued to see Billie, of course, and that had its own problems. Briar would cover for him as long as she could, but Adrian already suspected that his son was up to something "shady." He took to watching Craig any time he was on the grounds, and looking for reasons to keep him around the farm after hours. Briar countered, by asking him to go on errands for her that were essentially nonsense, and in that way her sudden bout of fatigue was turning out to be more of a benefit than a drawback.

Mickey sent gifts via Craig – nothing big, nothing that would attract Adrian's attention. He sent a new book about the Arabian horse; there was nothing suspicious about either Briar having that in her possession or about a friend sending it to her, even if her husband saw that friend as a professional rival. He sent a picture of Billie with Purple Reins from the Kingston Cup.

Briar was able to find a way to get to sleep after the first week, but it seemed as though her body wasn't able to catch up to its sleep debt. She found that she was sleeping at least twelve hours a day, not that anyone noticed but her, and when she did wake up the last thing that she wanted to see was any kind of food. She wasn't throwing up, but she did wind up feeling like anything beyond a little dry toast was well beyond her capability.

The thought that she might be pregnant did cross her mind, but she dismissed it. She and Mickey had used a condom; it shouldn't be a problem. No, she'd probably just caught some kind of virus in the press of people at the race, or maybe when they'd been out and about the next day.

By the middle of the second week, Briar started to notice pains in her breasts, toward the ends of her nipples. She wasn't going to pay any attention to that, not at all. She couldn't be pregnant, so the pain in her breast had to be from something else – a scratch she hadn't noticed getting, or a side effect of the virus. A quick Internet search told her that while the medical field was most concerned with breast pain and infections in breast-feeding women, child-free women or women who were not breastfeeding at the time could still experience breast infections. She was probably experiencing something like that; if the problem didn't resolve itself in a day or two she would have to go to her doctor and see about treatment.

As it happened, she let another week pass. She just couldn't make herself get out of bed. By the end of the week, she had to admit that her period was late, but that didn't mean anything. Everyone knew that you could be a little late when you caught a virus or something. Her entire metabolism was off; it only made sense that her reproductive system was a little confused.

Through it all, she got little messages from Mickey. They weren't anything that could get her into trouble, just little things. Sometimes they were just notes about his horses, or a selfie of him and Billie. Sometimes he sent the notes from Billie's phone, so they looked less suspicious. She deleted all of them; she couldn't take the risk of having Adrian find them. She did break down and reply to a few of the ones that came from Billie's phone, though.

Finally, a week after she first missed her period, she couldn't lie to herself anymore. Condoms weren't foolproof. They were mostly effective, but sometimes they were defective. Accidents happened. She might not have caught – there was still hope that it was just a nasty, lasting flu bug – but she knew that she needed to find out for sure.

She dragged herself out of bed and drove herself not into Middleburg, where the staff at the drugstore knew her, but twelve miles up the John S. Mosby Highway to the town of

Paris. No one knew her there, and she could buy the test in relative anonymity.

After it had been purchased, she ducked into a sandwich shop and picked up a bowl of soup. Once she'd choked half of it down, she sneaked into the bathroom and took the test.

Nothing could have been worse than those five minutes, as Briar sat in that semi-clean stall waiting for the test to finish processing her results. She tapped her foot. She chewed on her nails. She blew her curls off of her forehead. For the first time in weeks that roiling in her gut wasn't due to whatever stomach bug had taken hold of her.

When the timer went off, she stared at the results for a full five minutes. They didn't change. Briar didn't have a stomach bug. She hadn't picked up some kind of virus at the race. She was pregnant.

She threw away the test, and washed her hands. Then she went out to her car, turned on the radio, and cried.

When she'd been younger, she'd wanted kids. Not too many, no more than one or two, but she'd always hoped she could be a mother. She'd fantasized about daughters, about passing her love of horses on to tiny little girls who would – of course – look just like her. She'd imagined styling their hair before school, teaching them how to care for natural hair and teaching them to be proud Black women who could stand proud of their own accomplishments and those of their people.

She'd even had a boyfriend, her senior year of college, who had been on the same page with her. Joseph had been smart, and he'd been an agricultural student. Together they would have taken over her father's farm when he'd been ready to retire, and then she truly could have brought her daughters up in touch with the same horses and the same land that Briar herself loved.

That had all come crashing down the day that her father had called her into his office. Adrian Worthington had been standing there, his beady eyes riveted to her like they might have been to a new horse or an exceptionally shiny bracelet. "Baby," her father had said, "I'm going to have to ask you to break your engagement to Joseph." And he'd explained it all to her.

He'd traded her away like just another horse. She'd done everything for her father, worked on his farm from the time she was old enough to walk, focused her academic work on equine studies so that she could help build up the family business, and he'd gone and sold her to this creepy old man, older even than her own father.

She could see why he would. She'd known that her father was having financial difficulties, but she hadn't known the extent of them. By "marrying" his daughter to the man who held his debt, he would in effect be getting a fresh financial start. That was the only reason that Briar had gone along with the scheme. It didn't take the sting out of his betrayal.

Adrian had made it absolutely clear, as soon as they'd both signed the marriage license at the Justice of the Peace's office, what she could expect. She would live comfortably, and she would be expected to attend him as his wife at all public events and family gatherings.

She would have no role in his business, nor in his bedroom. Her role was purely decorative.

She'd had to abandon any idea of having children of her own. Adrian had two children by his late first wife, Craig and a daughter, Sondra. Briar couldn't even console herself with the idea of helping to raise those children, because they were older than she was. Sondra had children; Briar was technically their step-grandmother. Sondra had made it abundantly clear that she didn't have room in her life for a "gold digger" like Briar, and did not want Briar anywhere near her children. Both Briar and Adrian obliged Sondra without complaint.

So Briar had abandoned any hope of children in her life, and she'd made her peace with it. If there had been any possibility of convincing Adrian that the child she carried was his, perhaps the situation would be salvageable. As it was, this was an unmitigated disaster.

She'd done this to herself. Yes, they'd used a condom, but it wasn't as though she hadn't known that condoms came with a risk of failure. She had known better than to go anywhere near Mickey Ratcliff once she recognized that she was attracted to him. Maybe her life with Adrian wasn't all that it was cracked up to be. Maybe if she were free, she'd make a different choice, tell Adrian and his money that they could go to Hell and save her a seat, but as it was her behavior had consequences for people beyond herself.

Her stomach lurched, and she barely got the car door open before she was sick again. Her father was going to lose the farm. He was going to lose the farm, and he was going to lose it to cold, malicious Adrian Worthington. Sure, her father had sold her to Adrian to pay his debts, but he'd been left with little choice. Some bad business decisions had left him very short on cash when her mother had been diagnosed, and then her sisters needed help with college, and all he'd been asking for was the sacrifice of one daughter.

Even if he deserved to lose the farm, her mother didn't deserve to be out on the street. Her mother didn't deserve to lose her medication, either, or to lose access to the assistants that helped her with her day-to-day activities. Her sisters would be able to get through school with loans, but she'd rather not saddle them with that kind of crushing debt.

Not that she was going to have much choice.

She had one option: she could abort. She discarded that option almost as soon as it popped into her head, though. Sure, this baby was coming into the world under less than stellar circumstances, but she couldn't look at her conscience and say that she didn't want a baby. Maybe not right now, maybe she didn't know how she'd get through this, but she couldn't bring herself to seriously consider getting rid of it.

She did need to have a serious talk with Mickey, though. While she had the hard work to do, this child was his too, and he should have some input as to what happened with the child. She'd been trying to avoid this, having any kind of conversation with Mickey. It was too much of a temptation. Now that the worst had happened, though, the conversation couldn't tempt her to anything that could destroy her life any further.

She took out her phone and called his number. He picked up on the first ring. "Briar? Is everything okay?"

She couldn't help but smile through her tears. Mickey was such an amazing guy. If she'd met him five years ago, maybe none of this would have happened. Maybe the embryo in her belly right now would be a little brother or sister, instead of an only child and the fruit of adultery. "No," she said. "Not really. We need to talk."

"Where are you? I'll be right there."

She gave him the address and sat back to wait. He pulled into the space next to hers in a dark SUV with tinted windows – private, discrete. Subtle. She smiled at his intelligence as she popped a couple of breath mints and opened the passenger side door for him.

"Briar, you sounded awful on the phone, and I can see you've been crying. What's wrong?" He reached out and took her hand. "Did he say something, or do something?"

She chuckled. "No, not yet."

He turned to face her. "What do you mean, 'not yet?' Briar, what's going on?"

She took a deep breath. Her hands and feet felt like lead. She couldn't escape this. "I'm pregnant."

His face broke out into a wreath of smiles, genuine and unadulterated joy. She marveled to see it. How could he see a baby as anything but a hindrance, as an obstacle? Then he composed himself. "I take it you're not enthusiastic, and you're pretty sure it's not Adrian's."

"He's never touched me." Her words came out harsher than she intended, and she bit the inside of her cheek. "I'm sorry. I don't mean to be so snappish. Adrian and I have never been sexual with each other. You're the only one since college." She swallowed. "The baby is yours."

He laughed out loud. "I never thought I'd see the day."

Her eyes bulged. Had he somehow missed the seriousness of the situation? Had she been speaking Chinese when she'd told him about how Adrian had her whole family in the palm of his hand? "You're happy about this?"

Mickey sobered up quickly. "I appreciate that it's probably not as happy an occasion for you, and I'll respect whatever decision you make. But Briar – I've never had a family, you know? A baby, a child, that's mine – that would be real. A real family. And the fact that it would be your baby – well, that's pretty exciting too." He took a deep breath. "But whatever you want, baby. I'll stand by you, whatever you want to do."

Briar burst into tears again, and Mickey took her into his arms and held her until the tears stopped.

Chapter 5

Once Briar had finished sobbing her heart out and drenching the front of Mickey's dress shirt, he kissed her forehead. It didn't matter that they hadn't seen one another in weeks, or that she'd barely replied to his messages. He still kissed her like he cherished her, like she meant something to him. "All right," he said, pulling back for a second and grabbing his phone. "I'm going to have Billie come and get your car. Then we're going to go back to my place, okay? We'll talk about where to go from here, what to do. When you're ready," he said, patting her shoulder as tears rolled down her face again. "Not until you're ready."

"I'm sorry," she said, grabbing a tissue and dabbing at her eyes. "I'm not usually this weepy."

"Hey." He squeezed her hand. "If there's ever a time when a woman 'gets' to be a little emotional, it's right now, okay? And

I get it. This is throwing your whole world for a loop. But we will figure it out." He dialed Billie's number. "Billie? Hey, I need a huge favor. Can you get someone to drive you out here and drive Briar's car back to my place?" He paused. "Yeah. It's a big deal. Sure, if you think he'll be discreet. I knew I could count on you, Billie Bean." He hung up. "She's going to ask Craig to bring a few of your things over to my place later on, too."

"Oh my God, Craig!" She put her hand over her mouth. "What kind of a position am I putting him into?"

"Hey." He took her hand again. "Craig is a grown man – a very grown man, according to Billie – and he can make his own decisions. He's going to choose to help you, because he cares about you. So relax, sit back, and we'll wait for Billie."

She put her head on his shoulder and gave in. Anything that was going to happen, was going to happen. For now, she could be happy just sitting back and basking in all of the reassurance that Mickey had to offer.

Billie showed up half an hour later, hopping out of the passenger seat of a pickup truck blazoned with the Ratcliff Stables logo. She threw her arms around Briar without a second's hesitation. "I have no idea what's going on," she said, "but don't you worry. We're going to sort everything out."

"You're the best, Billie." Briar smiled for what felt like the first time in days.

Billie grinned at her. "I know." Then she laughed. "Now let's get you home. Kelvin misses you."

Briar moved over to Mickey's SUV, and Billie took over behind the wheel of Briar's BMW. "See you back at the ranch!" the jockey said, and lurched her way out of the parking lot.

Briar watched her go. "Does she even know how to drive stick?" she asked, wincing.

Mickey snorted. "She'll remember in a minute. Let's get going." He started the engine, and they were off.

Mickey's house stood on the top of a hill, reached by a tree-lined drive. The home that Briar shared with Adrian was magnificent, and it too was surrounded by the vast acreage that made up Adrian's farm, but the Worthington farm was new, cobbled together from farms Adrian had bought up and shut down. The main house was new construction, built after the death of Craig's mother, and while it was grand and impressive, it didn't inspire the kind of awe that the main house at Ratcliff Stables did.

Mickey hadn't so much purchased a farm as he had an estate that functioned as a working horse farm, and the centerpiece of that estate – to those who weren't involved with horses –

was the manor house. Briar wasn't an expert, but she would have to guess that the main part of the house predated the Revolution. Subsequent owners had built additions, of course, but they'd managed to keep the original character of the house intact, and Briar felt like she was driving up to some kind of nobleman's demesne instead of the home of a friend and one-night-stand.

He smiled when he saw her face. "Don't worry," he said. "Everything's been updated. I'm a big believer in modern plumbing and electronics, personally. I think there's a lot going for them."

Briar blushed. "Of course. I must really be showing my 'backwoods country girl' look today."

"Nah." He shook his head. "You should have seen me, the first time the realtor brought me to see it. Come on inside.

We'll get you situated. I can fix you some tea – decaf, I think we've got some good herbal stuff around here."

She nodded. "I'd like that."

He took her by the hand and led her indoors. From the outside, she'd have expected everything to be stiff and formal, but his décor turned out to be practical and inviting. For a moment, she could see a child – their child – toddling through the kitchen, waving a lollipop around and giggling like she'd gotten away with something.

She turned her brain away from the image. She couldn't think like that, couldn't think that far ahead.

Mickey led her into the kitchen, where a light-skinned woman smiled at her and shooed Mickey away from the stove. "I don't know what he told you, but if it involved the stove he lied," the woman told her. "The last time I let him near the stove he melted three pans. Three! Don't ever let him cook, my dear. Don't even let him near the grill."

Mickey just laughed and shook his head. "Ms. Jennings would have you believing that I've never survived a day on my own in my life. Briar would like a cup of tea, please. Herbal, no caffeine."

Ms. Jennings gave her boss an old-fashioned look. "And you're psychic now, as well as a trained cook?"

Briar laughed in spite of herself. "A cup of tea would be great, Ms. Jennings. Just – no caffeine. Whatever you have is fine."

Ms. Jennings bustled about putting the kettle on and chasing Mickey and Briar out of the kitchen. Lacking anyplace else to go, Mickey took her into a little sunroom. The glassed-in room had a stunning view of the surrounding countryside in general and Mickey's farm in particular. "Is that Kelvin?" she asked, pointing to a paddock not far away.

"It is. I think he's missed you. He won't let anyone else near him, not even Billie." He hesitated. "You know, no matter what happens, I hope you'll come over and help out with him. Right now, he's a handful, but the way you got him calmed down was so gentle, so masterful, that I think you might be the only way that we can realize his full potential. Otherwise, I'm not sure what we could do with him."

She bit her lip. "I'd like that. It just all depends..."

He looked away. "Yeah. I know."

"I mean, Adrian's going to lose his mind when he finds out. I'm really scared."

Ms. Jennings brought in the tea – one cup for Briar and one cup for Mickey. When she saw the way her boss' face darkened, she hurried right out again. "Do you think he'd hurt you?"

Briar frowned. "He's never raised a hand to me. I don't think he ever raised a hand to Craig's mother either. It's just..."

"Everyone knows how he is." Mickey folded his lips into a grim line. "Look. I know that you're scared. You're already here, and I'm not going to send you back to him if you don't feel completely, one hundred percent safe with him, okay?"

She sighed. "It's not me I'm worried about! It's my family! I didn't marry Adrian for myself, Mickey!"

He took her hand and pulled her closer to himself. "I know you didn't. How exactly did all that happen, anyway? I have to say, it all sounds a little pre-revolutionary to me."

Briar took a deep breath. "I know." She'd never told anyone the whole story before. She'd been pretty sure no one would care. Now, though, seeing the look on Mickey's face, she shrunk away. "I know. I let my father turn me into a prostitute and that's awful —"

"I'm not angry at you, baby. You did what you thought you had to in order to save your family. And that's fine. I'm proud of you, really. You've been so strong, all these years. You put that kind of responsibility on yourself, with no one to support you through it."

She smiled a little. "Craig's been a saint. He's been a rock, really. I don't think I could have made it this far if not for him."

"Well, it's not like I haven't seen the way his father treats him, either." He leaned forward and took her hand. "Briar, I want to do whatever you need for this baby. I told you before; I have always wanted a family. I never had one growing up, so the idea is just... well, it's just really, really appealing to me." He looked past Briar and out the window for a moment, and Briar got the sense that he was looking at a lifelong dream.

"I will do whatever it takes, whatever you need. You just want someone to pay child support and go about his merry way? I can do that. However much you want, whenever you want it. You want to live here, with me, as roommates who have a kid? Fabulous. I can do that too. You want to try to make something more work? Great. You want me to take the baby, raise it on my own? I'm here for that too. All you have to do is tell me."

Briar closed her eyes and pinched the bridge of her nose. "Mickey," she said, and stood up. "You don't understand – I barely know you, but I can totally see myself staying with you, raising our baby together." She felt her breath hitch and struggled to keep the emotions down. "I mean, even if we had nothing, and lived like my parents did. I know that you have the kind of heart that could give our child a good, happy family life."

"Damn straight," Mickey said, sticking his chin out.

"In a perfect world I would jump at the chance to raise our baby together. The problem is that my husband is holding my family hostage, and I can't – it's not fair to them. It was stupid of me to take that risk. I mean my mother can't get along without her medicine, without the helpers that come to her! Adrian will take all that away and worse."

"No." Mickey got to his feet. "I'm not going to let that son of a bitch destroy us, our child and my one chance at having a family. No way, not going to happen." He put his hands on her shoulders. "If you want this, Briar, and if you're willing to fight, then say so. Stay with me. Stay here, don't go back to that house that you hate."

"Mickey," she gasped.

He kissed her, heated and demanding and needy all at once. She yielded. Everything that she needed right then was in that kiss: love, and hope, and the passion she'd been forced to abandon all those years ago. "You'll stay?" Mickey asked her, eyes boring into hers.

She nodded. "I'm terrified of what he's going to do to my family, but I'll stay. I want this." She claimed his mouth in a searing kiss of her own. "I want you."

He cradled her face in his hands, tongue probing at her mouth until she let it in and sucked gently on it. "You've got me," he murmured into her ear, as his hand brushed across her clothed breast. "You've got me for as long as you want me."

She could feel his length, already hard against her leg and she liked that. She liked that she could get him hot and bothered and wanting, almost as much as she liked the way he got her worked up. She rubbed a hand across his broad chest and smiled to herself as he moaned. Maybe she'd been foolish, maybe she was taking a risk she had no right to take, but she was going to enjoy every minute of pleasure that came with it.

He unbuttoned her blouse slowly, shaking fingers having difficulty with the tiny buttons. "Do you have any idea what you do to me?" he asked her, still meeting her eyes. "Especially now that I know that's my baby inside of you?"

Two people coughed behind them. Briar squealed and Mickey yelped, stepping in front of Briar so that she could fix her shirt. "Billie! Craig! It's good to see you over here!"

Craig walked into the room first, followed by Billie. Billie looked like she was trying to stifle a laugh. Then again, Billie usually looked like she was trying to stifle a laugh. Craig's face seemed a little harder to figure out. "Well, that's one hell of a pregnancy announcement," Briar's stepson said.

"Um." Briar hung her head. "About that."

"You going to leave my dad?"

"I'm pretty sure I'd be out on my ear anyway, once he found out." Briar turned away. "I'm sorry, Craig. I didn't mean for this to happen."

"I know you didn't. And Briar – don't be sorry. I'm happy for you. Out of anyone who ever deserved to be a mother, who deserved to be happy, it was you, you know? I know that old sack of... I know my father wasn't going to let that happen. So congratulations." He hugged Briar so tightly that she thought she might break a rib. "Just put in a good word for me with your new man, okay? He can't ever have too many jockeys on staff, you know? And I could be good for training, too. I'm not a one trick pony." He winked at her and at Mickey.

"You're not mad?" she asked, falling onto the couch rather than deliberately sitting.

"No. I've loved having you around the house, but it's not like you were happy there. Anyone with eyes could see that. He just doesn't care. I'm going to follow your example, Briar." He sat down beside her and wrapped an arm around her shoulder. "I'm going to look for a new job, somewhere else. And as soon as I can find a job, I'm going to tell the old man where to stick it."

Briar had gone from terror to arousal to overwhelm in ten minutes. Neither her body nor her mind knew what to do with itself. "I... thank you, Craig. Thank you."

"You'll still be my best friend, though. Right?"

Now it was her turn to hug him. "We'll always be best friends, Craig. You can even be the baby's godfather."

Billie had to swoop in and claim a hug, too. "I'm so happy for you, Briar," she said. "I know this isn't the traditional way of doing things, but the three of you are going to make the best family ever. I guarantee it."

Billie and Craig stayed for dinner. Craig had brought a few of her clothes and things from Adrian's place, for which she was grateful. After they left, Mickey showed her to one of the guest bedrooms. "I'm sure you'll want your space," he said, shuffling a little. "I mean, I know we said we were going to do this together but…"

She couldn't hide her disappointment, although there was nothing disappointing about the room itself. It was large, and clean, and well appointed. "Thanks. It's a nice room." She bit back on the urge to make a snarky comment about goodnight kisses. "Thank you for all of this. I know you don't have to."

He bent down and touched his lips to hers. "I want to." He paused. "I really, really want to."

Now she did give him a wicked little grin. "Oh yeah?" She kissed him, a little deeper, and let her hands roam gently over his torso. Just like before, he let out a little strangled moan that had her entire body heating up. "Oh, that's nice."

"You like that?" Mickey grinned down at her and closed the door to the bedroom. "There's plenty more where that came from." He took his shirt off, and his undershirt, leaving her with what felt like acres and acres of bare skin to explore.

And explore she did. She explored with her fingertips, seeing as how she hadn't been able to touch him in almost a month, and she explored with her tongue. She loved the taste of him, the smell of him. Somehow ever since she'd gotten pregnant her sense of smell had gotten stronger and she could pick up on things she wouldn't have dreamed possible before. Mickey wore Old Spice deodorant, but that couldn't block out the scent of the stable. She could smell the hay on his clothes, the horses he'd ridden today, and the grass in the paddocks. As she licked her way across his chest and down toward his belly, she could taste the salt from a hard day's work and it made something warm pool deep in her belly.

She sank to her knees, tugging at his belt buckle. "You don't have to," he said, eyes kind and damp. He put a hand over hers, not forbidding but reassuring.

She smiled. "I want to." And she did. She wanted to give him this.

He took his hand away, and she freed his trapped, half-hard cock. She hadn't had the chance to do this the last time they were together. Now she rubbed her cheek against his member, getting a feel for it, trying to remember how to do this and make it good for him.

Then she went for it, taking just the head into her mouth and bobbing her head up and down until she'd taken as much as she could. She used her hand to cover what her mouth couldn't take, and she focused on making Mickey feel good.

If the sounds he was making were any indication, she wasn't doing a half bad job. He hissed and he moaned, and he groaned. He clutched on to the sheets, and he closed his eyes and breathed very deeply. Then he put his hand on her shoulder. "Baby, I have to stop you. I don't want to come like this."

She pulled off of him with a pop that made him whimper. "How come?"

"I want to come inside you." He guided her up and off the ground, leading her up onto the bed. "I want to come inside you when it's just us. Nothing between us. Since we can now."

She laughed out loud. She hadn't considered that little benefit to their situation. "Yeah," she said. "Let's do that."

She let him undress her. She'd always liked it when her partner undressed her, feeling like a present being unwrapped. This time was no different, although maybe Mickey had a little more appreciation for her than either of her previous lovers. With every layer that Mickey peeled back, he made sure to kiss, and rub, and pet, and suck, until she felt like her entire body was on fire.

She moved over to the edge of the bed to take him, and he stood on the floor with her feet on his shoulders. She grinned with anticipation. This position would be a little challenging for someone who had been celibate for so long, but he would be able to get so deep into her this way that it would be worth it. He met her eyes. "Are you sure about this, baby?"

She nodded. "Yeah. Please. I'm ready."

He lined himself up with her entrance, and then he slid home. His first couple of thrusts were gentle as he figured out just how much she could take. Then, he lost any ability to maintain control and pressed himself deeper, and harder, into her body.

Briar cried out. This was what she'd longed for. She had wanted to be filled up so badly, and Mickey was willing to do it. When he first began to thrust in earnest she'd just been able to hold on for the ride but after a minute or two she found the rhythm and was able to buck up and meet him thrust for thrust, even with the moans of pleasure that he was tearing out of her.

He gripped her hips and held them tight, a clear message, and she stopped moving as her orgasm washed over her. He, too, found his climax at that moment and they came together, moans quieting as they came down from their ecstasy.

They fell asleep in the same bed. Briar didn't care who saw or who found out. There was nothing she could do to change things now anyway, and she didn't want to.

In the morning, Mickey woke her with a kiss. "I need to go. I need to talk with my attorney, make sure that you, the baby and your family are safe. I'll see you tonight."

She fell back into a dreamless sleep, secure in Mickey's protective aura.

Chapter 6

Briar slept late; she didn't have a lot else to do. She dreamed about the possible life she and her baby could have with Mickey, here on his farm. She dreamed of holding a toddler's hand as the little one ran across the lawn, laughing happily in her headlong race toward Daddy. She dreamed of dressing a little girl up and doing her hair all pretty for her first day of school, complete with lots of little bows to show the world just how special and loved she was, while Mickey took pictures from the doorway and looked on with fondness.

She dreamed of teaching her daughter to ride. The little girl would be scared at first, but would get more confident with each passing day. They would put her on a steady, older mare, one that had long since passed any thought of jumping or bolting, and Briar's daughter would ride between her parents through the rolling hills of Mickey's estate.

Briar dreamed of her daughter's first dance, and of her daughter's first date. She dreamed of seeing her daughter off to prom, dressed in a pale pink gown that showed her dark skin off to perfect advantage.

She dreamed of bringing her daughter to college for her freshman year. She would cry when she dropped the teenager off, but she and Mickey would rest secure knowing that they'd raised their girl right and that she would make the right decisions. She could see them driving away from William and Mary, holding hands in the front seat and smiling at one another.

When she woke, she shook her head. What was she thinking? This was more than counting her chickens before the eggs were hatched. This was counting them before the eggs were even laid. Sure she wanted these things, absolutely. Now that she'd made a decision to try to work things out with Mickey and build a life with him and their child, she could start to think about the baby with happiness.

But thinking about the baby with pleasure and joy didn't mean that she and Mickey were going to have the kind of life that she dreamed about, not by a long shot. There were so many variables that she had to consider. They'd had one good night together. They had chemistry, he was a good man, and he wanted to do right by her and his child. That didn't mean that Briar and Mickey would be compatible as life partners. Sure he was open to the idea of building a life together now, but this had absolutely been an unintended pregnancy. What happened when he met someone further down the road, someone that he truly wanted to be with? He would resent her, and maybe the baby.

What was done was done. All she could do was sit back and try her best to protect her family, from her parents on their farm to the embryo in her belly. She *wanted* to make things work with Mickey, of course, but she wasn't foolish enough to think that it would just happen without a lot of work. She needed to be prepared for every eventuality, and not get hung up on romantic notions about True Love Forever.

She got up and took a shower, grateful for the warm water pounding down on her tense muscles. Last night had been incredible, but had only provided a temporary release from the anxiety that plagued her. The only thing that would truly help would be time, time and making sure that everything worked out. In the meantime, she could self-soothe with a warm shower.

After her shower, she went in search of breakfast. She wasn't sure what to do about that. She was afraid to leave the property, in case Adrian found her and forced her back to his house. At the same time, she didn't want to be presumptuous and start rummaging through Mickey's refrigerator.

Fortunately for her, Ms. Jennings was there to set her mind at ease. "There you are! Mr. Ratcliff said you were probably tired, poor thing. You just have a seat, I'll have breakfast up in a jiffy." The cook gave Briar a broad smile, no judgment implied at all, and bustled about the kitchen.

Briar shuffled over to a seat at the breakfast bar and obeyed, watching while the older woman busied herself getting breakfast on the table. "Have you worked for Mr. Ratcliff long?"

"No, just for the past six months, since he bought the farm. I used to work for the Suttons, up until Mr. Sutton passed, but it's good to be working here. Mr. Ratcliff's a good employer, takes good care of his people. He's not too demanding, either. He likes what he likes, don't get me wrong, but as long as you don't try to serve him something like ham or pork, he's happy." She beamed. "I like the place, too. The other workers, the horses. I work hard, but still – I'm pretty happy here."

"Do you live on-site?"

The kettle went off, and Ms. Jennings turned to pour two mugs of herbal tea. "I do. There's a little cottage on the property that I have, it's part of my compensation. It's nice – not too big, since it's just me, but I don't have to worry about traffic or anything. I think it used to be the coachman's house, a couple hundred years ago." She passed one of the mugs over to Briar.

Billie bustled into the kitchen. Briar wondered if the tiny woman ever just walked into a room, or moved slowly at all. No wonder she was such a successful jockey, she thought with a grin. Billie just couldn't move slowly, not even if her life depended on it. "Briar! You're up, fantastic. And Ms. Jennings is taking care of you. She's the best, but you're already figuring that out. I swear, there's not a better cook in Virginia."

Ms. Jennings waved a hand. "Hush. Leave poor Ms. Sharp something to learn, would you?" She flipped the omelet she'd been preparing for Briar and shook her finger at Billie. "And you – There isn't anything in here for you, do you understand me? Not until lunchtime."

"Yes, Ms. Jennings." Billie hid a smile behind her hand. "She raised five children alone, you know," she whispered to Briar as the cook turned back to her work. "You can't get away with anything around her!"

Briar's smile faded a little. Ms. Jennings had raised five children, and here was Briar freaking out about the possibility of having to raise one. Still, Ms. Jennings would be an excellent resource when Briar had panicky questions about the baby. She could see how good the older woman was, just by spending time around her. "How are things going today?" she asked, hoping to change the subject away from children.

"Not too badly," Billie said. "We got some good workouts in for some of the horses. Kelvin's still Kelvin. Hey, when your breakfast is done why don't you come out and take a look at him? He's restive, but you were so good with him the last time that it's worth a shot to see if he'll settle down for you this time." She crossed her hands over her generous mouth. "If you're not worried — I mean if you don't think that it's too dangerous."

"I'll be careful," Briar promised. "I've been dying for a chance to earn my keep around the horses for four years; I'm willing to give it a shot."

After breakfast, Briar followed Billie out to the stables. She still had a little bit of nausea, but now that she knew what was going on it didn't seem to affect her as badly and she was able to move past her early-pregnancy woes. They passed through the stables where Mickey kept his current racehorses, and where he kept the jumpers and dressage champions.

They passed the boarding stables and the draft horse area, and then finally they came to the segregated space where Kelvin was being kept.

Briar frowned. "Well I can see part of the problem right away. Horses are herd animals; everyone here should know this already."

Billie sighed. "Don't I know it." They watched the big chestnut foal for a moment. Kelvin watched them back. "He was starting to lash out at some of the other horses around him. I think he probably just needs more exercise, but Mickey wasn't willing to take that risk until we knew for sure."

Briar approached Kelvin. She moved slowly, hands out and visible, so that the horse would see everything she was doing and wouldn't spook. He stood still, not frozen, but watching. "Hey, Kelvin. You remember me, don't you, big guy? Yeah, it's Briar. Briar, from the track. You didn't care for the track, did you? No, you didn't. Too much noise, too many new things. Your old owners were foolish for making the exchange at the race; it was a terrible idea." She kept her voice low and measured, no sudden bursts of sound to startle the horse. In a sense, her pregnancy-induced lassitude was an asset here, because she couldn't work up the energy to shout or scream.

Kelvin sniffed at her hand through the slats on his stall door. Briar drew closer. "Is he tied to the wall?" she asked Billie.

"He is." Billie took a deep breath. "Let me guess – you want to let him loose."

"Well, I think he needs to run around a little. There's a ring attached to this barn, or at least a paddock, right?"

Billie nodded, already moving toward the stable door. "Yeah, you betcha. Let's do this."

Billie's quick movements didn't sit well with Kelvin, but Briar kept talking to him in a soothing, calming voice and kept his eyes on her. She took the lead rope when her friend got it attached to the cranky colt's bridle and led Kelvin gently out to the pasture, still talking gently to him the whole time

Once out on the pasture, she let him off the lead. Kelvin was off like a shot, running around the enclosure at full speed for several laps before getting down on the ground and rolling in the grass. He reared up on his hind legs, stretching and whinnying, and pawed at the ground before running a few more turns.

When his pace started to slow, just a little, Briar called to him. The first time she called, he ignored her. She called again, with more of a tone of command in her voice, and he trotted right up and nuzzled her shoulder.

"I can't believe what I'm seeing," Billie said, leaning against the fence as Briar fixed a lead to Kelvin's bridle. This was a lunge lead, the kind that was used to work Kelvin back in Kingsport. If Kelvin's behavior was going to improve, he was going to have to run out some of his energy, and Briar was going to help him do that.

Now that Kelvin had gotten a chance to get the excess energy out of his system, he turned out to be exceptionally eager to please. At least, he turned out to be very eager to please Briar. When Billie tried to step into the ring and take over he showed his displeasure by snapping at her and trying to step on her feet, but Briar regained control quickly and both women were able to laugh about it.

"When you two bought Kelvin," Briar asked, keeping her eyes on the horse, "did his old owners say how much training they'd given him?"

"Not really. I didn't think they'd given him any, but I can see that he's gotten some." Billie sighed. "Just enough to make him dangerous, I guess."

"Yeah, well." Briar snorted and encouraged Kelvin back up to a trot. "I have to wonder if he didn't just learn by watching. He's a very intelligent horse, and he wants to please, but he definitely thinks he's in charge. He needs a confident hand, but not an overbearing one. And he needs a lot of exercise. Way more than he's been getting, otherwise he's going to just cause trouble." She grinned. "I'd be happy to take that on."

"I'm a little nervous about having the mother of my child working so closely with such an unpredictable horse as Kelvin," came Mickey's smooth tenor from behind them. Both Briar and Billie turned around, startled by the horseman's sudden arrival. "Still, he does seem to trust you in a way he doesn't trust anyone else living. I wonder if I shouldn't be asking serious questions about the farm where I got Kelvin."

He folded his lips tightly and took off his hat. "I need to talk with you. Both of you ladies. In the house, if you don't mind."

Briar looked at Billie. Was this normal behavior from Mickey? The wide-eyed stare she got in return told her that no, this was not normal, nor did it bode well. Together, they got Kelvin back into his stall and summoned a groom to rub him down and get him some water. Briar would rather have done this herself, but it looked like Mickey's news couldn't wait, whatever it might be.

The two women walked into the house together. Billie held Briar's hand, providing much-needed reassurance and direction as they made their way through the huge old manor. Mickey had chosen to meet with them in the music room, a room Briar hadn't seen before but whose purpose couldn't be mistaken by anyone who walked in.

Some of the antebellum decor had been retained, such as the grand piano and the carved wooden music stands in various points around the sea-green room. Portraits of young white women in colonial and early American clothes, all playing music, hung on the walls, and Briar wondered if Mickey had bothered to change a thing in this room when he'd bought the place.

The room had received some updates. The piano still stood there, but a modern acoustic guitar sat before one of the antique music stands. Some modern recording equipment had been set up nearby, and a state of the art stereo system had been installed at the far end of the room. And of course the women in those portraits, or their ghosts, looked down at Briar and Billie and at Mickey, who sat on furniture they'd have only been allowed to polish even sixty years ago.

Mickey carefully took off his jacket and turned to face the women. Briar frowned. Her man, or however they wanted to define their relationship, looked tired. He looked tired, and his right cheek looked a little darker than his left. His knuckles had gotten scraped up somehow, too, and there was no reasonable explanation for how a grown man busted up his knuckles in the middle of the day.

Mickey took a deep breath. "So. I went out today."

Briar nodded. "You said you were going to see your lawyer." She squeezed Billie's hand. "To make arrangements about the baby." He'd said he was going to make arrangements to protect the baby, but she wouldn't blame him if he'd been looking to protect himself.

"And I did." Mickey scraped up a little smile for her, but the ends of his mouth just got pulled back down toward the floor as if by magnets. "I did. I sat down with my lawyer, Sal Montgomery, and we talked about our options. Then, then we drove over to Adrian's place."

Briar gasped. "You went to Adrian's? He knows I'm here?" She sprang to her feet, heart slamming against her ribcage in her panic. "Oh God – I have to go."

"Briar, calm down." Mickey turned to her.

"No, no, you don't understand. He's going to – I don't know what, but he's going to be so mad. I don't know what he's capable of but he's going to be furious." She clutched at her throat, as though that might help get more air into her heaving lungs. "He's going to destroy everything."

"He was mad." Mickey gave a little chuckle, and there was no humor in it. "He punched me in the face, actually. I gave as good as I got, though, and between Sal and Craig they got us separated and talking like adults. I'm not going to deny that Adrian was pretty angry. He said a lot of nasty things."

Briar's legs wouldn't hold her up anymore, and she sagged

back onto the couch. "He's going to kill me." She buried her

face in her hands.

"I can tell you one thing," Mickey told her, coming to sit beside

her. "When I saw the way he reacted, Briar – when I heard

the things that he said – there was no way that I was going to

let him keep you. No way I was going to let him have one

second of power over you, or our child, ever again. That man

is the devil. He's just… he's the devil. I don't know how

you've stayed so strong all these years, baby." He kissed her

forehead and wrapped her up in his big, strong arms.

She wallowed in the embrace. "But wait – 'let him keep me?'

You mean he wanted to?"

Billie patted her back with soft, gentle touches. "Yeah, that

doesn't make a lick of sense. His wife was pregnant with

another man's baby. Why would he not be happy to just wash

his hands of the whole problem? He's got two grown children he doesn't even want; he isn't going to be gung-ho about raising a third."

Mickey sighed, and held Briar a little closer. "Yeah. I asked him that. I swear, he could freeze over the lake of fire. He just said, 'Look, Ratcliff, that woman owes me. Her job is to be pretty and to make me look like a successful husband. A baby does that, and by law the child belongs to the man that owns the bed. I'm keeping that bitch, and that baby, and there ain't a thing you can do about it. She knows I've got her by the short hairs; she can't leave.'

"And he was just so smug about it, Briar. There was no affection. No concern for you. He never asked me if you were okay. He didn't even use your name once. He was mad, but it was more like he was mad because I took his sports car out for a spin." He shook his head. "I was just... I couldn't do it. And nothing I could say was going to make him budge."

"He thought he was going to trap Briar there and force her to stay with him and raise the baby as his?" Billie stopped patting Briar's back now. "What is wrong with that man?"

"Narcissism." Briar picked her head up off Mickey's chest now. "He's a control freak, and he's dangerously narcissistic. He would, too. He'd sit there and hold my family hostage just so he could control me. I don't know why. I still don't know why he wanted to marry me in the first place; it's not like we have a real marriage."

"I know, baby. I know." Mickey nuzzled into her neck, just as Kelvin had. "He's an awful man, but you're free now. I couldn't convince him by appealing to his heart."

"He doesn't have a heart," Billy said, tossing her head. "Craig could have told you that."

"I believe he said words to that effect, yes. But since I couldn't get to him through his heart, and I couldn't get to him through good sense, I went after him through his wallet."

Briar felt cold, all of a sudden. "You bought me."

Mickey sighed. "It was the only way to get you away from him, Briar. I paid him money to relinquish his claims against you and your family." He shifted and reached into his briefcase. "Look. This document? Shows that your family's debt is paid off – not just set aside, but wiped clean. No one can hold that over your head, and make you do anything anymore. This document here," he continued, pulling out a sheaf of papers, "sets up a trust to provide for your mother's long-term care needs, because I don't trust your father to not try to do some more shady dealing. I don't mean to cast aspersions on your daddy, I know he was just trying to do what was best with what he had available, but daughters are not bargaining chips." He looked down at Briar. "Who knows? We might have one on the way ourselves."

Briar softened, and stroked his face. "You did all this, for me? And the baby," she added quickly.

"Mostly for you, though." He grinned, and then his face fell. "There's just one drawback. It's kind of a big one."

"What is it?" She held her breath. "Is he going to force one of my sisters into my place?"

"No. He can't do that anymore, not to anyone in your family. I can't stop him from going after other people's families, I suppose." Mickey took a deep breath. "He wants a new jockey." He swallowed. "A star."

Billie shook her head. "No."

Briar's mind spun. Mickey had done that – had betrayed his best friend – for her? She couldn't conceive of it. Still, it wasn't fair to Billie. Billie wasn't just Mickey's friend. She was Briar's friend too, and she was Craig's girlfriend. And she wasn't even being given the illusion of choice in being sacrificed to Adrian's ego.

Mickey pulled back and rubbed at his face. "The thing with athlete contracts, Billie, is that they're bought and sold. Or traded." He looked away, unable to meet the eyes of either woman.

Billie rose to her feet. "I cannot believe you." She stormed off toward her suite.

Briar rose. Mickey put a hand on her shoulder. "I had to do it," he said. "I didn't have a choice. I couldn't leave you there, Briar. I couldn't."

"I know." She kissed him. "Thank you. She's hurt, and I get why. But – you'd take her back, right?"

"In a heartbeat, but there's nothing to be done about it."

Briar smiled. "Leave that to me."

Chapter 7

Briar followed Billie up to her suite. She wasn't surprised to find the jockey had a suite to herself; she knew that Billie and Mickey had been best friends since childhood. He could probably have provided her with a proper house on the property, if either of them had wanted to, but somehow she doubted that either of them had even considered it.

Part of her knew that she should think twice about trying to build a family life when there was another woman involved, especially another woman who was so very close with her man. Briar had never been the jealous type. Even if Mickey and Billie had tried to go there once, something she saw no sign of at all, she knew that Billie was head over heels for Craig anyway.

Huh. Was forcing Mickey to give Billie up some kind of twisted attempt on Adrian's part to act like a father and help his son out? It was twisted and surreal, but it fit with the way that Adrian approached life.

Briar shook her head. No, Adrian wouldn't have been thinking of Craig. He only thought of Craig when he wanted to blame someone else for his own failings.

She knocked on the door. "Billie? Billie, it's me."

Billie threw open the door, face as angry as a herd of spooked wild stallions, but her fury collapsed as soon as she looked at Briar. "I should kick your ass away from me," she told Briar. "But I can't be mad at you. It's not like it's your fault; you didn't send him over there to do this."

Briar stepped into the suite. The space was minimally furnished, which made sense. Billie traveled a lot, and she hadn't had a lot of time to put her own stamp on the place yet. "No. I didn't. And I wouldn't. I don't like this, one bit. You and me, we're both being treated like the horses."

"Worse than the horses," Billie said, flouncing over to the sofa. She glanced over at Briar. "Especially you; you've been dealing with it longer. It's all new to me. I expected better of him."

Briar sat down beside her friend, turning to face her. "I have to admit that I was thrown for a loop. I don't think he'd have agreed to it if it weren't for the baby. But Billie, it's not the end of the world."

Billie's pretty face twisted. "It's not? You just escaped from that man's nasty clutches and you think it's not the end of the world? I know you've seen how he treats his employees. I know you've seen how he treats Craig, because you're usually the one bringing him the ice packs."

"Well, he's not going to lift a hand to you because you'll slap him with an assault charge faster than you can spell 'charge'." Billie raised an eyebrow. "I don't know about Adrian's contracts specifically, but I'm pretty sure that most courts will release you from your contract if he's been convicted of assaulting you. But Billie, that's not why I'm telling you that it isn't the end of the world."

Billie snorted and turned away. "Oh, what, you'll name the baby after me? That makes it all better while I have your jackass of an ex-husband in my face screaming at me for twenty minutes about how my hair is an eighth of an inch out of alignment?" She got up and stomped into the bedroom.

"How could he do this to me?" she raged, throwing things into a suitcase. "I have been here for him, through everything. Everything! Every setback, every sudden move, every win. Everything he has, he has because we won it together."

"It's true." Briar pulled the haphazardly thrown clothes out of the suitcase and folded them neatly. "I'm not pretending that it wasn't a lousy thing to do. I think it's eating at him. Here's the thing. I know, for a fact, that Mickey's horses are better than Adrian's. Marginally better, but that little tiny bit makes all the difference in a race. Right?"

Billie didn't want to hear her, but she stopped and listened anyway. "Go on."

"And you're the best jockey on the circuit right now. Everyone knows that. But even you can only do so much." Briar gave Billie her sweetest smile. "I was thinking, on my way up here, that maybe Adrian was trying to help Craig out by forcing you to come and work for him but no. No way. In his mind, you and me? We're not people. We're things, to be bought and sold just like the horses, or like used cars.

"As soon as Mickey came on the scene, Adrian started losing more races. And then, he lost his trophy wife. In his mind, Mickey stole something from him. Mickey stole his reputation, and when Mickey stole first place Mickey 'stole' money from his pocket too." Briar rolled her eyes. "By forcing you to go work for him, Adrian thinks he's going to steal the money back from Mickey. All you have to do…"

Billie stared at her for a moment and blinked. Then, realization dawned. "You want me to tank races." She shook her head. "A jockey who tanks races will never work again."

"Only if you get caught. You're good enough that all you have to do is hold back a tiny bit. Come in second. Let Adrian micromanage the horse and don't say anything when the horse gets a stone under his shoe."

"Is that what happened in Kingsport?"

"That's exactly what happened in Kingsport. Just… sit back. When Adrian realizes that he's not winning any more races than he was before, but he's still got to pay your high salary under the terms of your contract, he'll be begging to terminate your contract. And Mickey will be more than happy to sign you a new one." Now Briar's smile turned wicked. "And if that contract happens to have a no-trade clause in it, well no one could possibly blame you."

Billie leaned back. "Really?"

"First of all, you and Mickey are best friends. He'd never say no. He doesn't want to let you go now. Secondly, he'd be a fool to let the best jockey in the sport walk away if she wanted to come back, right? And Mickey Ratcliff is many things, and a fool is not one of them." Briar smiled then, showing teeth.

Billie chuckled. "True. How long do you think that Adrian will stick it out?"

"No more than six months. He's angry, which makes him impatient." She smirked, and settled back against the couch cushions. "It's going to be hard. I'm not going to lie. It's going to be hard, because he's going to be in your face twenty-four seven and he's going to say all kinds of things about you.

Things that will have you wanting to punch him in the face. You can do this. We can do it together."

Billie hugged her. "We can. Thank you, Briar. You're brilliant."

The next day, under the terms of the trade agreement between Adrian and Mickey, Billie went to Adrian's farm. She was given an apartment in one of the outbuildings, where she was expected to reside, and she didn't say goodbye to Mickey.

She did take her leave of Briar, though. And she left most of her things in her suite at Mickey's house, which Mickey said he took as a good sign.

Briar found a good obstetrician, thanks to Ms. Jennings recommendation. Dr. Prakash was friendly, smart, and didn't come at her with a lot of nonsense about a "special time" or "delighting in the purpose of your body." She addressed Briar by her name, never reduced her to "Mom," and spoke to her like an intelligent human being instead of like some kind of overcooked turnip.

The first race that Billie rode for Adrian was in New York, up in Saratoga, two weeks after Billie left. Briar and Mickey were there as well, as was Craig. Billie came in third, Craig came in fourth. Purple Reins came in first again, although his time wasn't as good as it had been at Kingsport. Mickey fretted about that, but they both knew the reason.

The four of them got together for dinner that night, although out of courtesy for Briar no one drank. "He's worse than I thought he'd be," Billie said, slumping in her chair. "I have to admit that I kind of want all of the horses to spook at once and trample him." She winced and glanced at Craig. "Sorry."

"Why? I'm not." Craig squeezed her hand. "Would you believe that he locks us in our rooms at night to make sure that we don't get up to any 'hanky panky?' Those are his words. 'Hanky panky.' In this day and age. We're in our thirties!"

Mickey's laugh was a little strained, but he made the effort. "I don't think he's updated his vocabulary since he was ten," he said. "You know, when Billie comes back, there's an open offer for you to come with her. The contract is sitting in my desk drawer. I'd email it to you but I don't want to get you in trouble."

The racing papers were forgiving of Worthington Stables' loss. Adrian, Briar knew, was less so. Billie called and told her about the dressing down she received, both for that and for the dinner she and Craig had enjoyed with "my adulteress wife and that prick who sleeps with married women."

"He got right up in my face, in front of everyone else in the stable," she told Briar in an exhausted voice. "I think he expected me to cry."

"You didn't though."

"Hell no I didn't. He doesn't know me." Billie laughed through her fatigue. "I gave it right back to him. I lit into him about the condition of the horse I'd been on, I lit into him about locking me into my room like some kind of prisoner which was not in my contract, he will be hearing from my attorney by the way, and by the way he is not entitled to have any opinion on who I associate with during my off hours."

"Good for you," Briar smiled. "I don't think he's ever had an employee who he hasn't been able to control before. I don't think he's going to like it."

"Good. I hope it gives him heartburn."

Briar's episodes of morning sickness passed, and she started to recover some more of her energy. This gave her more time to work with Kelvin, and she spent time with some of the other horses as well. She also started planning the baby's room, an activity that gave her and Mickey a lot of pleasure.

The next big race was in Maryland, a month after Saratoga. Billie came in second for Adrian, with Craig coming in third. Mickey ran a different horse in that race, on behalf of a friend of his in Dubai, and that horse took first. Adrian was so angry that he was shaking, and the racing journals got unflattering candid shots of that. They also got unflattering candid shots of him unloading at Billie, and being unloaded at in return by Billie, which made the front page.

Briar rubbed her hands together as she sat over her breakfast the day after they returned from the race. "I hate that poor Billie has to put up with that man," she said to Ms. Jennings. "I have to say, though, that the plan is coming together nicely."

"Mmm." Ms. Jennings raised an eyebrow at her. "Wasn't there any other way to make this happen?"

Briar sighed. "Not by the time I found out about it. Probably not, knowing Adrian. I wish that we could have done it without sending her over there, but – well. If wishes were horses, I guess."

"Yes." Ms. Jennings glanced at the picture. "I would not want to be that Worthington fellow. Billie looks like she's going up one side of him and down the other, doesn't she?"

"Serves him right." Briar took a sip of her coffee.

Billie lost the next two races. She came in second, and made a great showing, but just didn't bring in the kind of prize money that Adrian would have been hoping for. Briar watched from afar, keeping her fingers crossed every time that she sat in Mickey's box and watched a race.

Briar's body started to change. Initially, her breasts swelled by a full cup size, which she certainly didn't mind. Mickey didn't mind that either. By about the fourth month, though, Briar couldn't deny that she was showing. Her baby bump wasn't huge but it was pronounced, and she couldn't decide how she felt about that. The baby was responsible for changing her life for the better, but would Mickey still want her as she grew more swollen and misshapen?

Mickey did. Mickey took every opportunity to shower her with affection, to be the anti-Adrian. He kissed her cheek every time he passed her. He held her hand, and he kept his arm around her shoulder even when they were in public. He made sure that everyone around her knew that they were together and they were in love.

She never had a reason to doubt how he felt about the baby, either. He was initially hesitant to make suggestions about the baby's room, but after Briar took him by the hand and said,

"Hey – this is your baby too," he became less shy about showing his enthusiasm.

"Public or private school?" he asked her one day.

"I went to public school," she said. "I had a good experience. I'd rather put her in public school and move her if we have to than just assume that the public schools are bad, you know? But if you'd rather put her in private, if you've got strong feelings about that…"

He laughed. "You've got some pretty strong notions that the baby's a girl."

She blushed and ducked her head. "Well, I don't like calling her 'it.' I'll be happy as long as the baby's healthy, but I just don't like saying 'it'."

"We can say 'she' until we know," he told her, passing a hand over her belly.

It was funny to Briar, that she liked it when he touched her belly. She hated it when other people touched her there; she was starting to hate it when other people touched her at all, as though her status as an expectant mother somehow made her public property. But Mickey, she loved it when he passed his work-roughened hands over her burgeoning belly. It stirred something very deep inside her, some kind of desire that she didn't think she wanted to look at too closely.

They still slept in separate bedrooms. Briar didn't think too much about that. She'd had her own room when she'd lived with Adrian, and from what Craig had told her Adrian's first wife had her own bedroom. Maybe people at this level of wealth just expected to have their own rooms. Maybe that was just their normal. She could live with that.

It wasn't what she wanted, but everything else was working out so well, she'd learn to live with that.

Billie lost another race, and a reporter for one of the racing papers cornered her outside the ladies' room. He asked if he could ask some questions, on the record, and she gave him an innocent smile and said, "Sure, of course."

The article that followed made even Briar wince. The headline said, in huge letters, WORTHINGTON CONTROL FREAK! The substance of the article got worse from there. According to the article, quoting liberally from Billie, Adrian was a control freak who micromanaged every aspect of his employees' lives right down to the underwear they wore. Which would be fine, she said, but it obviously wasn't getting them results.

He was worse with the horses. Not only did that create a negative environment for the horses, leaving the horses fearful and skittish, but it had created an environment where none of his employees would open their mouths to tell him when there was a problem. "My horse in yesterday's race had a stone in her shoe. I knew it. I tried to say something, but he insisted on inspecting her himself and insisted up and down that everything was fine and that there were no problems. Said that if I tried to make any changes before the race he would fine me for insubordination.

"Now I hear he's trying to ruin my reputation. He's accused me of trying to throw races. What possible benefit could that have for me? The man is unhinged. He's such a control freak that it's hurting his business, hurting his bottom line, but he can't admit that so he's looking to blame a woman. But ask anyone in that stable. They'll tell you. Hell, just stand back and watch."

She showed Mickey, who grimaced. "He's not going to be happy about that. I mean it's all true, except the part where she really is trying to throw races, but she could have been a lot quieter about it."

"Maybe." Billie bit her lip. "We're in a very conservative business. There are still a lot of people who believe that women don't have any place in a stable at all, except maybe around dressage."

"True. Your charming ex-husband is one of them."

She nodded. "Billie, in being so very outspoken, while being the absolute best, I think might call some attention to that. Also, people are going to take a much harder look at Adrian's business now. They're going to think twice about having him as a trainer, about having him as a breeder."

"True enough." He kissed her. "Don't we have an appointment today?"

She nodded. "The big reveal. Are you ready?"

He took her hand. "Ready as you are. I'll be happy as long as the baby is healthy."

Together, they drove out to Dr. Prakash's office. The doctor sat in the room with them while the ultrasound technician got her equipment ready. Briar bared her belly while Mickey held her close; the room was chilly, because the equipment needed to be kept cool, and Mickey knew she'd be uncomfortable.

It took the ultrasound tech a moment to find anything, and Briar felt a brief moment of panic. Dr. Prakash patted her hand and smiled. "Don't worry. Your placenta is in the front, which is why you're not feeling any kicking yet. I listened to the heartbeat in the office, remember? Your baby is very healthy."

Just then, the tech found what she was looking for. The creature that appeared on screen didn't look like a baby, but Briar could see where things would grow into baby-like parts. The tech pointed to blobs on the screen. "Okay, here we go. Here's the head up here, it's looking good. Over here we have two arms, two legs, we have eyes, and it looks like things are developing normally at this stage. Now the big question: do you want to know the sex?"

Briar and Mickey exchanged a long look. "We do," he said after a moment. "It doesn't technically matter, we'll be happy with whichever, but we don't like referring to our baby as 'it'."

"You're going to be the parents to a beautiful baby girl," the tech told them, and printed out the sonogram pictures.

Briar cried tears of joy, and the tech and the doctor rushed out to give them some privacy. "A daughter," she said, as Mickey wiped the ultrasound gel off of her belly and helped her to cover up. "A girl! I always wanted a daughter."

Mickey hugged her close. "This is amazing. I'm so happy right now." He cleared his throat. "She's going to be so beautiful, Briar. She's going to look just like you."

"I hope she looks like you," she whispered, looking up at him. "Come on, let's go home and talk about names."

They drove home, already discussing the different possibilities. They both liked Wilhelmina for a middle name, in honor of Billie, but they wanted her to have a unique identity given that Billie was going to play such a strong role in their daughter's life. Billie suggested Rosa. Mickey countered with Harriet. They considered Laverne, but thought Michelle might be a little more modern.

When they got home, they found Billie's car in front of the house. "This could either be very good or very bad," Mickey said, parking the car and helping her out.

The pair raced to the door and into the music room. There, sitting on the couch, were Craig and Billie. Billie wore a giant grin on her face, and an even bigger diamond ring on her left hand. Craig's smile was sheepish, but still happy.

Billie sprang to her feet. "Guess who just got bought out of her contract today?" She jumped forward and threw her arms around Briar. "That's me, by the way. He tried to fire me outright, but I called up Sal Montgomery. Sal was more than happy to talk to Adrian. At length." She laughed, head thrown back and eyes closed. "He had to buy out the rest of my contract, because Mickey here never put a 'no media' clause in my contract and Adrian was so eager to buy my contract he never read it. Ha ha!"

Briar hugged back. Nothing in the world could feel as good as this day.

Chapter 8

Rosa Wilhelmina Sharp-Ratcliff was born on March 15, at 4:18 in the afternoon. She weighed eight pounds, four ounces and was twenty-two inches long. She entered the world through Caesarian section, due to some complications that arose as Briar neared her due date. Briar had been a little nervous about a surgical delivery, but when the risks were explained to her she agreed with Dr. Prakash that it was better to be safe than sorry.

She spent four days in the hospital after Rosa's birth, healing and learning to care for the precious new life that had just come into the world. Rosa wasn't like other babies in the maternity wing of the hospital. She cried, but she didn't wail, and she didn't cry if there wasn't something that could be handled immediately. Most of the time she wanted Mama, and that was just fine by Briar.

Rosa might have a preference for Mama, but she certainly didn't mind Daddy either. She liked to cuddle right up to him and fall asleep on his chest, with her knees tucked up against her chest and her tiny hand on his face. He ate it up, too, never wanting to give her back to her Mama until she squealed.

They brought Rosa home on the fifth day. The hospital staff all gathered around to say goodbye, and Briar couldn't help but feel a little teary at the separation. These people had helped her over the past few days. They'd been a rock, a mainstay on whom she could rely ever since she'd been wheeled in after the surgery. Now she was going to go back to Mickey's house, and she was going to be on her own.

Except she wasn't, not really. She was going back to Mickey's house, where Ms. Jennings was waiting for her. If she noticed something about Rosa that gave her cause for concern, she could just ask Ms. Jennings. Billie would be there, too, willing and happy to lend a hand or a shoulder to cry on. Craig was there, anxious to be Uncle Craig once again.

And, of course, Mickey. Rosa's daddy, and the man with whom Briar had fallen in love.

She felt ridiculous. Mickey was nice. He'd really stepped up and taken care of her ever since she'd told him that she was pregnant, and he'd gone the extra mile for Billie and Craig too. He'd been great toward her as a lover, too, never showing the slightest loss of interest once her body started to change. Anything that had needed to be done, Mickey had done or he'd paid to have done, and Briar couldn't think of a single way in which she'd ever been better cared for in her life.

They still slept separately, though. Maybe he didn't want to make their romantic relationship long-term. Maybe he'd give her a residence on the ranch, let her have a job as a trainer or something. She'd be content with that. She'd never sought a life of luxury, and as long as she got to keep her wonderful Rosa with her she'd never utter a word of complaint.

It wasn't Mickey's money that she wanted. What she wanted was him. Now that he had gotten the baby he wanted, would he have gotten sick of her?

These were the thoughts that tumbled through her mind as Mickey helped her out of the hospital and into his waiting SUV. He carried the bucket carrier with Rosa in it, since her incision still wasn't healed enough for her to lift the carrier with the baby in it, and he strapped her into the car seat with all of the concentration of a man trying to diffuse a bomb. Then he helped her climb into the passenger seat and even buckled her seat belt for her.

Once they were ready to go, Mickey leaned over and kissed her lips. "It's the first day of the rest of our lives, Briar. Ready?" And then he smiled.

Part of Briar, the insecure part that still thought he might be sick of her, quailed at the implications of that statement. The rest of her relaxed and squeezed his hand when he reached out and took hers. This was the first day of the rest of their lives.

When they got to the house, Craig and Billie and Ms. Jennings were waiting for them. They'd decorated the entryway and the path up the stairs in pastel pink bunting, and strewn pink and white balloons everywhere. Briar gasped, and Mickey laughed out loud. "Did you know they were planning this?" Briar asked him.

"He did not," Billie told her, bounding up to peer at the new arrival. "Oh my goodness would you look at her? She has your look of eternal annoyance when you wake her up. Aren't babies miraculous?" She poked at Rosa's little hand, and the baby grabbed onto her finger and squeezed. "I think she likes me."

"And what's not to love?" Craig came up and gave his fiancé a kiss on the cheek. "You're her auntie, you have to teach her everything her parents don't want her to know about."

"That's right," Billie said, tickling Rosa under her chin as the new parents groaned. "That's my job!"

Briar took her daughter out of the bucket carrier and brought her into the sitting room, tired after so much excitement. Rosa responded to the change by gurgling once and falling asleep. "It's hard work, being new," Briar told her child, stroking the baby's tiny face and kissing her little forehead. "You get your sleep while you can."

"Pretty soon you're going to want to be up all the time, not wanting to miss a thing." Ms. Jennings winked. "I have to say, the two of you make beautiful babies."

Briar blushed, while Mickey gave a little laugh. "I think we do. I definitely think we do." He cleared his throat. "Briar, I was wondering if I could ask you a question."

Briar glanced up, but she had to train her eyes back down. Mickey was getting down on one knee. "Oh my goodness, Mickey, what are you doing?"

"Briar, the past nine months have made me the happiest man alive. Not just because you gave me Rosa, but because you came into my life. You came into my house and shared my life. You shared my passion, you shared my friends. You've helped to grow my business and you've made every morning a happy one. Seriously, Briar, it used to be that I would wake up and sometimes I'd be so lonely I could just cry. Now, I know you're here. In this house, with me, building a life with me.

"I want you to keep building. With me. " He licked his lips and swallowed hard, and then he reached into his pocket. "I want to make it official." He pulled out a ring.

"You want me to…" Briar couldn't move her eyes from the diamond.

"Marry him," Billie translated. "For real. I know you haven't had the best experiences, but I think this one will turn out better."

"I didn't want to ask while you were pregnant," Mickey admitted, blushing. "I didn't want you thinking that I was just asking because of the baby. I wanted you to understand, to really get, that I want to marry you for your own sake, because I love you. Not just because of traditional values." Ms. Jennings glared at him and stomped on his foot, and he coughed. "Which are important, even if we've gotten them a little turned around."

Briar blinked back tears. "Yes." She nodded. "Yes, yes. Yes yes yes. I will – I want to marry you. It doesn't have to be a big or fancy ceremony or anything but I want to be your wife. And I want to point to you and say, 'That's my husband.'" She wiped at her eyes with her sleeves.

"No fair beating us to the bunch," Billie teased, dabbing at her own eyes with a tissue. "You've already got us beat on the baby thing. Which is fine, we've got time." She held up a hand and laughed.

"We can wait," Mickey said, hugging both women. "I wouldn't dream of trying to steal your thunder, Billie."

*****

Billie and Craig had a June wedding. It was the talk of the racing community. Briar was the matron of honor, and she worked very hard to get her body back into shape for the event.

She hadn't planned on hiring a nanny to help with Rosa, but she found that she'd taken on enough responsibilities with the stables and with some of Mickey's charitable endeavors that having someone around to help out just made sense. Fortunately one of Ms. Jennings' daughters had experience doing this kind of thing and was available. Rachel Jennings was smart, pretty and a writer. Looking after Rosa on an as-needed basis while Briar took care of other things around the property worked well for her as well as for Briar.

So Briar had the flexibility to get ready, and was now in shape to walk down the aisle in a champagne-colored gown that hugged every curve. Her bouquet of red roses was simple and pretty, and she felt like a million dollars as all eyes turned toward her.

Most of the guests knew her in one way or another. Some knew her as Adrian Worthington's distant, silent bride, but the people that knew her that way who had shown up here would probably also know more about Adrian's personality by this point. More of them knew her as Mickey Ratcliff's fiancé and partner. Others just knew her as Billie's friend, and a very rare few recognized her as Ricky Sharp's oldest girl. Everyone was staring right now, and she didn't care.

She looked good. She could hold her head high and know that while she'd made a few mistakes, in the end she'd done what was right for her child and for herself. She'd done right by Billie, too. Billie had gotten caught in Briar's mess, but Briar had come up with a plan to help her friend get out of it.

Briar made it to the front of the aisle. She turned around to watch Billie, being escorted down the aisle by Mickey. Mickey was also the best man, but this was an unconventional friendship and after everything they'd been through together Briar didn't think that anyone had the right to say anything to them about it. Billie looked stunning in a blindingly white strapless A-line dress, the kind that they showed in wedding magazines. Even Briar's breath caught for a moment, and she'd helped Billie pick the thing out.

At the end of the aisle, Billie passed her bouquet over to Briar, took Craig's hand, and turned to face the priest. The old man hadn't been open to the idea of writing their own vows, which the couple understood; he was an old-school kind of priest, but a good soul who loved them both and they were willing to go through with the ceremony his way. He said a prayer over them both, and then did the readings. Then he went through the Eucharist and only then, finally, could the couple exchange vows and rings.

Briar struggled to keep a straight face. She didn't know how Billie could breathe in that thing, standing still with her head bowed like that.

Finally, the Mass was over and Craig could kiss his bride. The wedding party processed out of the church to much applause and scrambled into limousines that would take them to the reception site.

The reception was at an historic inn in Middleburg; Billie had chosen it based on its elegance and its lack of proximity to anything horse related. "We all love horses," she said. "With the exception of the Jennings, horses are our jobs. All of our jobs. It's our day off."

Most of the guests enjoyed cocktails while the wedding party dealt with the hassle of photography. One of Ms. Jennings's daughters busied herself bringing drinks to the wedding party so they wouldn't be left out, while Ms. Jennings kept an eye on Rosa. Rosa, at her age, mostly wanted to grab onto shiny things and drool a bit, but she did make some memorable grabs for some people's drinks. She had learned how to give adorable smiles by now as well, and the wedding photographer captured a few of them for posterity.

The reception went smoothly, just as it ought to. Mickey gave an inspiring speech about both the groom and the bride; Briar gave a shorter speech but one that was equally heart-felt. The dinner was not quite so delicious as one of those that Ms. Jennings would prepare, but it was still more than edible and the red meat was a rare indulgence in the Sharp-Ratcliff home.

It was only when the dancing started that the slightest hint of trouble marred the reception. The bride and groom had just finished their first dance when Briar noticed someone from the inn staff arguing with someone just outside the function room door. She grabbed Mickey and went to investigate – that was their job, as the heads of the wedding party. The bride and groom didn't need to be bothered with trouble on their special day.

The person darkening their doorstep turned out to be none other than Adrian Worthington. He brought himself up sharply when he saw Mickey, a sneer of contempt marring his features. "I should have known that you were in this up to your eyeballs, Ratcliff. My son would never have pulled a stunt like this if it weren't for you!" He caught sight of Briar standing just beyond Mickey. "Whore."

Briar rolled her eyes. "You aren't welcome here. You need to leave."

"No whore gets to tell me that I'm not welcome at my own son's wedding!" Adrian's voice rose to a bellow and now Briar cringed. She'd wanted to avoid a scene, but instead she'd caused one.

The music cut out, and every guest stared at the doorway. Craig marched right through the crowd of dancers, Billie trailing right behind. "You have got some nerve, showing up today." Craig spoke through clenched teeth, and his hands were balled into fists at his side.

"I am your father. I have a right to be at your wedding, such as it is. I certainly didn't give my permission, and I don't approve of the skank you married." Adrian's lip curled. "What the hell makes you think that you have the right to pull a stunt like this? To give this harpy the Worthington name?"

"The right of a free man, over the age of twenty-one." Craig was a small man, but he met his father's eyes squarely. "You weren't invited, because you are not part of our lives. You made that pretty clear when Billie had to call a lawyer on you for breach of contract." He gave a thin, grim smile. "Billie has agreed to marry me in spite of the Worthington name, not because of it. Now. You have three seconds to get the hell out of here, before that nice gentleman in the apron picks up the phone and all the trainers and owners and jockeys here see the mighty Adrian Worthington arrested for trespassing at his estranged son's wedding."

Craig turned his back. Billie's face shone with pride as she, too, turned her back on Adrian. One by one, the other guests returned to their previous activities. The DJ even started the music up again, so that only Briar, Mickey, Adrian and the happy couple could hear Craig begin his countdown. "One."

Adrian turned to Briar. "You! This is your fault!"

"Two."

Adrian left.

The reception picked up right where it left off. Craig didn't speak of the interruption again, not that night and not at any point in the future.

Later that night, after the reception was over and the happy couple had been happily seen off to bed, Briar buckled Rosa into her car seat. "Do you think that we'll ever be like that?"

Mickey shook his head. "Nope."

"Why not?"

"Because we love each other." He closed the door, escorted Briar to her seat, and then got into the driver's seat. "Craig has told me, and I know he's told you, Adrian never loved his first wife, Craig's mom. He might have had some affection for Sondra; I've never met her so it's hard to say. But you and me, we have real love, baby. We weren't looking for it, but we found it. Nether of us could ever turn into Adrian."

She sighed and reached across the center console, taking her fiancé's hand in her own. The light from a street lamp caught on her engagement ring, reflecting in the diamond's facets filling the stone with an almost mystical light. "Promise?"

"Promise."

*****

Mickey and Briar married in August. They considered doing what Billie and Craig had done and having a church wedding. Briar's first wedding had involved no ceremony or joy whatsoever and Mickey wanted to give her that.

Briar wanted that, she did. She just didn't necessarily feel comfortable doing it in the same way that Billie had. Sure, they could get away with having their wedding in the church, but neither she nor Mickey were particularly religious and they'd gone and had the baby before the wedding. She didn't feel that she needed that – not for them, not at that point.

Instead, they opted for something much smaller. They brought Craig and Billie, and Ms. Jennings and Rachel, Sal and a handful of other close friends and associates, and brought them down to a beach in Newport News. It was a long trip, but the beach was worth it.

Briar wore a simple white sundress – not too long, so that it wouldn't get sand or seawater in it. Her natural curls waved in the breeze, and she turned her face up to the smile as she balanced Rosa on her hip. They'd talked about maybe having Rachel watch her during the ceremony, but both of them felt that it was important to have their daughter in the ceremony. She had, after all, been instrumental in bringing them together.

The minister, who had come with them from northern Virginia, smiled at them. His words wouldn't be long. "Dearly beloved, you have been asked by Briar and Mickey to bear witness to the official building of a new family. The foundations of the family were laid some time ago." Briar blushed, and a few people gave a nervous giggle, but the minister put a massive hand over Briar and Mickey's joined hands and smiled.

"That's not exactly what I meant. Yes, they did make a baby, and that gave them the incentive to start a family, but millions of people make babies together and wouldn't know a family if they tripped over one. I pity those people. Briar and Mickey, they knew that they needed to do something for their child, and so they made a commitment to build a family together, for that child.

"And along the way, they found love. Those are the two building blocks that you need, to build a strong family. They're the two basic factors that people have always needed. Love, and commitment. With those two basic structures in your hearts, everything else will build on that. Faith, hope, trust, compassion – if you have love, and you have truly committed to making this work, then those things will fall into place."

The minister squeezed their hands, and Briar looked up into Mickey's eyes. She'd made a commitment to this man. And yes, she loved him. She'd loved him before she knew that she loved him, but there was no reason to deny it to herself anymore. She loved Mickey, she wanted Mickey, and now she was going to share the rest of her life with Mickey.

The minister beamed down at them. "Do you, Mickey Ratcliff, take this woman, Briar Sharp, to be your lawfully wedded spouse? To have and to hold, to love, honor and to cherish, in sickness and in health, so long as you both shall live?"

Mickey's voice shook as he responded, eyes shining. "I do."

"And do you, Briar Sharp, take this man, Mickey Ratcliff, to be your lawfully wedded spouse? To have and to hold, to love, honor and to cherish, in sickness and in health, so long as you both shall live?"

Briar took a deep breath. "I do." There wasn't a moment of hesitation in her voice.

"Then, with the power vested in me by God and by the Commonwealth of Virginia, I now pronounce you man and wife. You may now kiss the bride."

Mickey took Briar into his arms and kissed her chastely on the lips. Rosa grabbed Mickey's collar and tugged, giving a mighty shout. "I don't think she likes PDA," Briar laughed, resting her head against his shoulder as Rosa fumbled for her teething necklace.

"That's okay, Briar. We've got time." His smile was brighter than the sun. "We've got the rest of our lives."

The end.

If you enjoyed this ebook and want me to keep writing more, please leave a review of it on the store where you bought it. By doing so you'll allow me more time to write these books for you as they'll get more exposure. So thank you. :)

Get Free Romance eBooks!

Hi there. As a special thank you for buying this book, for a limited time I want to send you some great ebooks completely **free of charge** directly to your email! You can get it by going to this page:

www.saucyromancebooks.com/physical

You can see a the cover of these books on the next page:

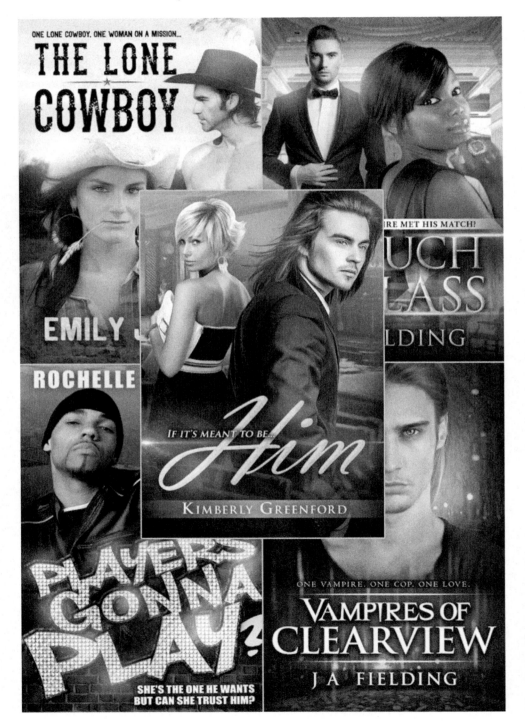

These ebooks are so exclusive you can't even buy them. When you download them I'll also send you updates when new books like this are available.

Again, that link is:

www.saucyromancebooks.com/physical

Now, if you enjoyed the book you just read, please leave a positive review of it where you bought it (e.g. Amazon). It'll help get it out there a lot more and mean I can continue writing these books for you. So thank you. :)

More Books By Ashlie Brookes

If you enjoyed that, you'll love The Billionaire's Marriage Of Convenience by Ashlie Brookes (sample and description of what it's about below - search 'The Billionaire's Marriage Of Convenience by Ashlie Brookes' on Amazon to get it now).

Description:

Leisha is a social worker doing vital, but under funded work in Syracuse, New York.

She loves her job, but it unfortunately doesn't leave much time to socialize.

Furthermore, her love life is non existent.

So when her old college roommate Amelia calls her out of the blue, it seems things might just pick up.

Amelia, now a high-powered PR exec, has a weird proposition.

It involves marrying Carlton Manning, the billionaire that built his empire from the ashes of his child star past, but now has some public image issues.

Leisha always had a 'from far' mini crush on Carlton.

So if they end up working closely together to improve his image, will that crush turn into something more?

Or will the reality of the situation mean their marriage of convenience is destined to fail?

Want to read more? Then search 'The Billionaire's Marriage Of Convenience Ashlie Brookes' on Amazon to get it now.

Also available: Dance, Lust And Them by Leonie Miller (search 'Dance, Lust And Them Leonie Miller' on Amazon to get it now).

Description:

Hip hop dancer Janelle has slowly been making a name for herself in the industry, and things are starting to pay off. Thanks to her ruggedly handsome 'friend with benefits' Curtis, she's just landed a job on Vance Quick's dance team. Vance is a famous singer who can have any girl he wants, though when he meets Janelle he only gains eyes for her. But with Curtis still on the scene, which man will she choose? Or will she find a solution where she can have them both at the same time?

Want to read more? Then search 'Dance, Lust And Them Leonie Miller' on Amazon to get it now.

You can also see other related books by myself and other top romance authors at:

www.saucyromancebooks.com/romancebooks

CPSIA information can be obtained
at www.ICGtesting.com
Printed in the USA
LVOW04s1524030616

491122LV00018B/688/P

9 781530 930487